Too Many Women

Now it would be fair to say that I have more experience than most men with the gods and their ways. One thing I have learned is that they really only have one joke.

Men laugh at many things, from 'A centaur and a sphinx walk into a taverna...' to a sad-faced clown chasing a dog running away with a sausage. I'm partial to a good mimic myself. The gods, however, seem to find humor only in pretending to be human. Thus have many entertained them unaware, except for the consequences which may be hilarious to the god in question but tends to end short and sharp for the mortal. Maybe that's the best part of the joke.

The ragged stranger who happens to drop a pair of winged sandals. The lovely girl who offers good advice on how to dispatch a monster. The old woman sitting by the side of the road?

"Have you come far today, Grandmother?"

"Very far. Any distance seems long when you are alone."

"True. That's why I'm looking for the girl."

She chuckled or choked on phlegm. It was hard to tell. "I saw her," she admitted. "Pretty little thing. Dazzled these old eyes."

I recalled another crone I'd met who turned out to be the Goddess of Love herself in disguise. I suppose if you could look like anything or anyone, you'd get a certain amount of entertainment out of it.

THE STONE GODS

Book Two

Eno the Thracian Series

C. B. Pratt

The Stone Gods
Copyright © 2013 by C. B. Pratt
Amazon Edition
ISBN # 978-0-9908754-6-8
All rights reserved.

CHAPTER ONE

After the third week of a one-week cruise, the sea had lost its sparkle.

I stood atop the mast, feet braced on the cross-bar. The *Idyia* wasn't the largest ship afloat and, sailing alone in the midst of a watery desert, she seemed even smaller. The mast transcribed circles with the motion of the sea below me. As I spun slowly, I surveyed empty sky and empty sea.

From time to time, I caught sight of the crowded deck. The crew, muttering, clutched staves, knives and axes. Some few clutched their heads, taking no further interest in me. Considering that the water ration had been cut the week before so that there was no more for washing, I was just as glad to be up where the air was fresh, even if they hadn't been trying to kill me.

By the second week of our one-week cruise, their camaraderie had begun to fracture. One or two had determined that the voyage had somehow incurred the wrath of some sea spirit or other and, in time-honored fashion, had looked about for a scapegoat. As usual, they'd picked on the only stranger on board. Me.

When the water ration had been cut the first time, they'd found ears willing to listen to their theory.

Today, with their captain face-down drunk on the deck, the knives had come out. It was climb or swim. I was secure enough for the moment, though I couldn't be sure that they were sane enough to refrain from chopping down the mast.

"Come down, Thracian!" The first mate, Nacrolos, had joined with the crew rather than be tossed overboard himself. A burly-chested man, he had a voice like the roaring of a lion, easily heard over winds and storms.

"You should see this view," I called back.

"We won't hurt you, if you come down."

True, that. Nobody wanted to anger a sea spirit or god further by spilling blood on the deck. They'd agreed that the best thing to do was to throw me overboard and leave my fate in the hands of the Moirae sisters. Those three alone knew whether my thread of life foretold my death on this day or another. If I drowned, my blood would not be on the crews' hands as it was evidently my lot in life since before my birth. I had objected for several reasons, not least among them was that drowning was no death for a fighting man.

The sun was a blurred white dot in the height of a pale sky. The sea dazzled with a thousand glittering shards until eye and mind alike were wearied. But beyond all that, I thought I glimpsed something else. I gripped the mast tight between my knees, to bring up a hand to shade my eyes, straining to bring what I saw into focus.

"You can't stay up there forever," Nacrolos said, adding to the others, "Thirst'll bring him down soon enough."

"I'm serious," I shouted back. "You should see this view. Send somebody up here."

After a certain amount of bickering and shoving, Nacrolos himself started up, climbing like a monkey or a sailor bred to the sea. Certainly better than I could do.

Clinging to the mast, braced against me for balance, he snarled, "What game are you playing, Thracian?"

He wasn't as tall as me, so at first he couldn't see it. Then I got a hold of his broad leather belt and hoisted him up, raising him with one arm above my head. He gasped, scratching and beating at my hand like a fool. The crew below cried out, thinking I meant to dash him down.

Then I felt the start he gave right through his belly as his wildly rolling eye caught sight of what I'd brought him up here to witness, a thing that haunted the nightmares of sailors since the dawn of time. "Do you see it? Do you?"

"By the mother of the gods...."

"Gods or not, that's the mother of all whirlpools," I said, lowering him 'til I could look him in the eyes. He'd gone green under his walnut-colored tan. "And we've been riding the rim for days, I'd wager."

"Aye. What's to be done?"

"We start by not throwing me to the waves."

"Of course not," he said, mindful perhaps that I had plenty of strength left. "Let's call that a joke, eh?"

"Let's call it a bloody stupid idea. The only thing keeping us riding the edge of this whirlpool is that somehow -- by the luck of Heaven -- our weight is neither too much nor too little. Throwing a weight like me overboard would change that by enough and then you'd really know what a curse is."

Nacrolos wasn't a fool when his thoughts weren't clouded by fear of the unknown. As we climbed down, he was already planning our escape. He thrust a meaty fist into the jaw of the first crewman who charged at me. Even as the poor fellow went down like a felled ox, Nacrolos shouted orders. "We man the oars, boys. And row, damn your eyes, as you've never rowed before."

They cut holes in the hull, carefully husbanding the wood to make extra oars. Though the crew continued to throw suspicious glances at me, having something tangible to do gave them heart to work with a will. They made a port for every man, saving no one for a second shift.

Pausing a moment in his work, Nacrolos took me aside. "I'm uneasy about this. If it goes wrong, we've had it."

"We've got to do something. Can't just keep sailing in a big circle 'til we die of thirst."

"I wish the captain were awake. He's a clever man; I'm just an old salt."

"At least you're still on your feet." I clapped him on the shoulder. "We'll be all right. I'll get back up there and tell you which way to steer."

"If there were only two of you...I'll need your strength at the oars as well."

In the end, we sent two men up the mast, one to sit on the other's shoulders so he could see the dark, swirling pit of water on the very edge of the horizon. We dared not steer for even one instant in that direction. As soon as we were broken free of the current that carried us endlessly around, we might meet any kind of wild water. If we were unlucky, we'd be swept down into a crushing oblivion of roaring sea and splintered wood.

I did not speak my fears to Nacrolos. There are two things in this world that cause a whirlpool. One is an influx of mixing waters. The other is a monster. We were far from the narrow strait haunted by Charybdis the Vast but there were other creatures almost equal to her brutality.

Of course, monsters make up a good deal of my business. My sign in the Athenian acropolis says it all really. *Hero for Hire. All monsters dispatched from carnivorous geese to Minotaurs. Special rates for multiples. Eno the Thracian at the sign of the Ram's Head, one flight up.*

But this brief journey from Athens to Kalithanos wasn't supposed to be for business. I'd taken down my sign and told my landlord to send any clients to Kyex, a nice fellow and a good fighter. If they didn't want to see him, they'd have to wait until I got back from visiting my mother.

Frankly, I'd rather face a hydra with a head-cold.

Not because she was so formidable, though she could fell an ox with one glance, but because the questions I had for her could easily be interpreted as insulting. Just how did one go about asking a decent woman whether she'd made a slight mistake and passed her infant son off on her husband, knowing he was not the father? Even my extra time on the *Idyia* hadn't given me an answer to that.

An hour into our labor, the captain woke up, staggered to the side and vomited like a volcano. Straightening up, he wiped his mouth with the back of his hand. Nacrolos started toward him to explain what we were doing. Before he reached him, though, the captain spewed again.

There's nothing more eye-catching than a man being deeply and thoroughly sick, as much as we might feel our own throat burn with a sympathetic gagging. Everyone watched him for a brief space of silence, then we all felt the change in the ship. A deep lurch as the ship, lightened by just so much, changed position toward portside, where the vortex awaited. "What in Hades' name was that?" Captain Eosphorous demanded.

Nacrolos explained urgently. The captain rubbed his no-doubt aching head as he tried to understand. "So what you're saying is...I should try to hurl *on* the deck?"

The lookout shouted down that we'd changed position and not for the better. The sailors redoubled their efforts, driven harder by their new fears than by their hope of escape. One by one, the thudding of axes ended as the sailors stood by at their ports, little more than a row of holes in the fabric of the ship. Captain Eosphorous, pale and sweating but in command, took his position where all could see him. He raised the padded drumsticks above an empty barrel laid on its side and gave the beat for the rowing.

The beat was low and urgent. We threw ourselves on the oars, driven by that thrumming which seemed less in the ear and more from someplace inside that warned us to 'hurry, hurry, or you'll be caught!'

At first, it went well. We broke from the current that had held us in place for so long. Two or three men raised a ragged cheer when word came from the lookouts that we seemed to be putting more distance between us and that swirling mouth of doom on the horizon.

The muscles stood up on our arms and backs like armor-plate as we strained to force the *Idyia* onward. Some men gasped for breath while others groaned with each pull. Their hands, sea-hardened though they were, began to run with blood, the red trickling over their bodies as they leaned back with the stroke, but not a man faltered. Even the two ship's boys, sharing an oar, fought with every bit of their power against the sea.

One of the lookouts came down to tell the captain, face to face, that they were losing. The whirlpool was nearer, close enough to be seen to port without even raising on tip-toe. We were wasting our time and our strength to no purpose.

I shipped my oar. Ignoring the inquiring cries of my shipmates, I went forward. Nacrolos followed me. "What are you doing?"

"Tie a loop in this rope for me," I said, pushing the coil into his hands. "I like to travel by ship, but I have no idea how they work."

"D'ye mean to hang yourself?" He tied a loop like a noose and held it out.

"Make it bigger, man. I'm no lightweight."

I stepped up into the bow. The *Idyia* was a newer vessel and lacked the high prow of the old ones. The front end extended farther from the ship and still bore the traditional 'living' eyes on either side. I could only hope that she would watch over me as I tried to save her life.

"Tie each end to those bits over there."

"Very well," Nacrolos said, as one who humors a crazy man.

When I slipped the loop over my head and around my chest, the excess rope coiling on the deck beside me, he tried to stop me as one confirmed in his estimate of my mental health. "It's suicide, Thracian. Come back to the oars where your strength is useful. With you, we might succeed. But if you do this, you condemn us all to die."

"It's in the hands of the Fates, don't you think?"

"Gods! Is this your vengeance?"

I shook my head. "Shout to tell me which way to go," I said and clapped him on the shoulder.

I dove over the prow, swimming fast to get ahead of the ship. The ropes grew taut as I found the proper distance. Then I began to plow through the water, throwing my arms forward without stinting while I kicked like a dolphin. With every stroke, I prayed as hard as ever I had in my life. To Poseidon, to Amphitrite, to Tethys, to every god, goddess or Titan who'd ever so much as admired a seashell. "Let there be no monster, let me be strong enough, let this damn well work."

Above the roaring in my ears and the splash of my efforts, I heard Nacrolos bellow that I should turn to starboard. "Not too much!"

I tried to make myself as mindless as a sail, as biddable as a rudder. I emptied myself of thought, aware only of the harsh voice crying instructions.

They told me later that there'd been a solid wall of water forever circling the whirlpool and that we broke through it as though it were made of glass. But don't believe it. We passed through no such wall on the way in. Legends grow like that, though. One day, no doubt, I'll hear the tale told and won't recognize myself at all.

They had to haul me out by the ropes, unable to make me understand that my task was done. I lay on the deck like a gaffed fish, choking up water. Somebody gave me a swig of wine that went down like fire. I'd gone from scapegoat to the most popular man on the ship in a matter of hours. Captain Eosphorous himself massaged my arms and shoulders with a preparation of his mother's that took away my soreness, though it left me smelling like a very dead gull.

We came into Kalithanos port on the morning tide. It took a while to say my good-byes. The captain refunded my passage fare so I had a little extra jingle in my pouch as I went to seek a bathing house where I could rid myself of the odor.

Almost at once, I met a nice young fellow who offered me his sister at half-price. "You're too generous," I said. "But if you happen to know a girl who speaks Maedi...?"

"Why, several." His eyebrows rose like a pair of caterpillars on an unexpectedly short leaf.

"It would be pleasant to make love in my own language. I've been among the Greeks for several years."

He laughed, showing gaps in his brownish teeth. "Sentiment! I respect that, sir. Wait here."

Going inside, I sat down on a bench. I was grateful to be off the constantly moving ship, though the earth beneath my feet hadn't stopped dancing yet. After a few minutes, the owner of the bathing house came over to me, a beaker in his hands. "You are a soldier?" he said in decent Greek as he poured out the wine.

"No. A hero."

"Eh?"

"A hero for hire. But I'm on vacation. Family business."

"Ah, I see." He waved to his assistant. The boy showed me through to the baths. He threw buckets of water over my body while I rubbed myself clean with a bag of herbs. Then into the plunge, to let the troubles of the trip fade from my muscles and my mind. But now that I was here on my native stones, the prospect of confronting my mother with my question had brought back all my tension. I emerged from the baths clean, but not relaxed.

"Are you making a long stay in Kalithanos?" the owner asked next, as he stropped his razor. "I have a pleasant suite above the bath here. Very convenient. Very cheap."

"No, I don't mean to be here long. Does the young man I sent from here have a place for his clients?"

"Yes, not so nice as my rooms, not so quiet, but good enough for the purpose. He is a trustworthy fellow. He works for Petta and she always has the best stock."

"Petta? Who is she?" I asked, spitting out lather.

"Runs a string of about fifteen girls or so. Doing very well out of it, this being a seaport and all. It is funny, you asking for a Maedi girl. She's one herself, or so they say."

There was no more time to ask questions as he waved the razor about under my chin. The Greeks are funny in that they think, or choose to believe, that everyone wants to be Greek. Their city-states have evolved to the point where they need only war with each other, which sometimes they did for land or to avenge an insult or, as it might seem to an outsider, something interesting to do during the long dry season. Naturally, they assume everyone wants to live the same way. If it's good enough for them, why wouldn't it be good enough for everyone everywhere?

Thrace, my country, is a place of steep hills, deep green valleys, and lots of sheep. Ruling the sheep are various tribes, more or less nomadic, following the grass-times as they flow up the mountains in spring and down again to the valleys in winter. However, to call Thrace a country, as the Greeks do, isn't exactly accurate. It is a place where tribes live, mostly in harmony with one another and with the land. They do not think of themselves as a nation with any single aim or center.

My tribe is the Maedi and Kalithanos was the first city of size I'd ever seen when I'd come out of those hills as a well-grown lad of about seventeen. It was a Greek transplant, clinging to the shore like a limpet. It had spawned no others farther inland. Thracians prefer tents to huts and clear pools to bathing houses. We do like wine, not being entirely opposed to all the benefits of civilization.

The bathhouse owner finished my shave just as the young man returned. He bowed low. "My mistress finds she has no girls that speak Maedi except herself...a favor not extended to all who ask it."

I flipped a coin to the bath keeper and followed the tout through the streets. A cool wind had sprung up, bearing with it a taste of rain. We passed through the marketplace, a teeming, bustling center where the incoming trade from the islands met with the entire output of goods of every land between the sea and the distant and half-mythical land of Chin. A hundred tongues could be heard in half a street and you could buy just about anything. If you didn't like the price at one stall, walk five steps and be met with a different one.

I caught a scent, strengthened by the on-coming rain, of a kind of sausage sizzling on a brazier sending up a thin blue smoke. The smell and sight set both my taste buds and memory working. I turned aside to buy one.

The tout appeared at my elbow. "Come, sailor. My mistress will feed you. It is included in the price."

"You don't know how much I can eat," I said, biting into the hot sausage. The skin snapped and the juice burst into my mouth, rich with green peppers and red spices. I laughed, knowing I was home.

Nodding to the sausage-man, I saw him put another on his grill. In Maedi, I asked him for the rough red wine of the high country. He snapped his fingers at his boy who trotted obligingly across the street. I popped the last of my first sausage into my mouth and waited eagerly for more. In my haste to get clear of the stink of the captain's special ointment, I'd forgotten how hungry I'd grown during my days at sea.

Waiting for the wine and my next bite of sausage, I looked to see where the boy had gone. In that idle instant, I felt eyes upon me. That is a sensation I am used to. When you top most men by a head and half, and are broad in proportion, you get used to curiosity. But a fixed and prolonged stare will still raise the hackles on my neck.

Among the tribal herders in their shaggy vests and uncured goatskin hats stood a strange figure, lean and tan. He wore a gold collar flat against the base of his throat, the scarab in the center enameled in green. The striped linen cloth bound about his brow echoed the plain linen kilt around his hips. His only concession to the cool climate was a short woven cape on his shoulders. Even his eyes were thickly outlined with black kohl as if he stood beneath the burning sun of Egypt, instead of a rain that couldn't decide whether spend its life as a drizzle or work hard enough to graduate into a full-blown storm.

I blinked and he was gone. Had he been a mirage sent straight from the desert?

I ate three more sausages, sending the boy running for another beaker, then paid the old man well. "You remind me that a man may be too long away," I said in our language. It's not elegant but it speaks well of homely things.

"I am too old to climb our hills anymore," he said. "But you are right even so."

The House of Eros stood in a side street, a stone's throw from the marketplace. Close enough for a man to take his pleasure and be back at his stall before his boss or his wife knew he was gone. The facade was relatively plain, except for a little dirty graffiti scrawled across the planters, praising Petta's speed and flexibility. Good advertising, I suppose.

The tout showed me to a room where I could strip off my clothes and wait. There was a table spread with sweet cakes and more wine. I munched a bean cake but I'd drunk quite enough for now. I did not disrobe.

I smelled her before I saw her. Attar of roses is not an inexpensive scent. Business must be good if she could afford to drench herself in it.

She all but oozed into the room, her draperies of finest linen revealing nearly as much as they concealed of her lush figure. Hair of a peculiar brassy blonde, the effect of using sulphur, saffron and honey to dye naturally dark hair, had been piled up in a tousled birds-nest. She blinked at me good-naturedly. "My, you're a big fellow...."

"Petta?"

"Who else?" She sighed and kind of shook everything into place as she came forward. Spreading her hands out over my chest, she leaned in.

"Not...Erkimyn? Of the Tents of the Piebald Goats?"

She stopped, blinking up at me, when she heard the name she had in childhood. I realized she had grown short-sighted as she squinted, trying to bring me into focus. Then she forgot her affectations and her business, screeched, "Eno!" and threw her arms around my neck.

CHAPTER TWO

She'd been a skinny child, her hair in a mat over her face, always tagging after the boys. Once she'd slid down a hillside, chipping her two front teeth across.

The body, the hair and the name had changed beyond recognition but the teeth were just the same. It gave her smile a certain girlish charm that she would never lose.

She reclined on a gilded couch, languidly fanning herself. "I'm always too warm," she complained. "Night and day."

Her body servant put a shallow rock crystal cup in her hand, by no means her first wine of the evening. "Pretty thing," she cooed, though I wasn't sure if she meant the servant or the cup.

"You have done well for yourself, cousin."

"I can't complain. At first, you know, you think you'll never sink so low. But when you are left alone in a big city by the only man you've ever loved...." She sniffed, batting her eyes as she considered whether or not to cry, and took another drink instead.

"In Athens, courtesans are well-respected members of high society."

"Here, too, I suppose. Early training tells though. You remember my mother?"

An Amazon in everything but birth. "Yes, I remember her very well. My ears still ache on cold nights."

Petta laughed. "They were her favorite handles. I think my right is still longer than my left. But if she knew how I make my living...."

"Have you been to the mountains lately?"

She shook her head, the curls bouncing. "I've never been back. She told me not to go with Pocik and washed her hands of me when I did."

"Then you haven't heard news from our people either."

"I didn't say that. I heard when she died."

"Gods," I said. "I'm sorry."

She tossed her head. "Don't be. It was her own fault. The judges wanted to stop the bout in the fifth round but she wouldn't listen."

To cover my confusion, I peeled a grape.

She began to talk of other things. She'd grown interested in collecting ivory carvings and she sent her servant to bring a sample of her collection for me to see. In our moment of privacy, she leaned forward to touch my knee. Despite the wine, her eyes were sharp as they looked me over. "Are you going back there? Up to the tents?"

"Yes, it's been a long time. My own mother...."

"She still lives, or did when I got my last word from up there this spring. There's been some kind of trouble. Not so many caravans crossing the high passes as once there was. No one seems to have much to say about why, only rumors of dark happenings."

"What kind of rumors?"

Her ample shoulders moved under the straps of her gown. "Ghosts...demons. Different things. But it's more than rumors, perhaps. I used to send a caravan of my own until it and all my men disappeared. Maybe they robbed me and are living happily with their harems in Samarkand. Maybe they are dust at the bottom of a ravine. If you go, be wise and go around the Black Mountain, not over it."

"I certainly will consider your advice. Can I carry anything for you on my way?"

She laughed, exposing a neck still young and unlined. The kohl and lapis on her eyes and her heavily rouged cheeks had made her look older but I remembered that she was younger than I. "I have no more money to waste on goods that never arrive. I will trade by sea until the passes open again."

I agreed that was probably wise. "What are you doing with yourself, Eno?" she asked, leaning forward to choose among my grapes.

I explained that I was making good money in my chosen profession.

"But you haven't gone to Troy? I would have thought there was money to be made, hand over fist, in the midst of a fight like that. First on one side; then on the other."

"I owe no loyalty to any of the cities fighting and no one has offered to pay me to change my mind."

"Ah, you are wise. Why fight over a straying wife? He should have taken her back to Mycenae when he had the chance instead of hanging around Sparta."

"The king resigned in his son-in-law's favor. Would you have him turn down a kingdom?"

Petta laughed again, this time at male folly. "Helen was raised in the drabbest, dullest, ugliest court in all the islands. When she had the chance to be married away and go elsewhere, her foolish father gave the kingdom to her husband. I don't blame her for running off to Troy first chance she had. Anything probably looked better to her than spending the rest of her life right where she'd always lived. Besides, they say Paris is a handsome lad. But if I'd been her, I wouldn't have waited. I'd have been off with the first shepherd...well, Hades, that *is* what I did!"

For a moment, she seemed to be reminiscing about her girlhood. Then she tossed her curls and shrugged off the past. "Well, a war can't last forever. Maybe they'll all come to their senses soon."

"I hope you're right. It's already been two years. Though it's been good for business, I hate to think of all those men away from their homes for so long."

With all the big-name heroes off in Troy, I'd gotten more work than ever, though my last job had left more questions in my mind than answers.

"Do you need a temporary job?" Petta asked. "I know all the richest men in town. No doubt one of them needs a body-guard or bouncer."

I declined with thanks. Petta was one of those women who couldn't do enough for you, so long as it required no real outlay on her part. She'd give me a meal or a girl, speak a good word for me among her clients, but not a demi-obol or silver spangle would she give away.

"I have more than enough," I said, tapping my money pouch. And it was true, now that I had my ship money back again.

The servant returned with a tray of carvings. Petta had nice taste, though she was more interested in describing what good bargains she'd made than in the artistic quality of the pieces. I lifted up an ivory figure of Isis suckling the infant Horus that was lightly touched with gold.

"Tell me, what are the Egyptians doing here? I didn't think their arm reached so far."

"I don't know much about them. They bring their own girls, we barbarians not being civilized enough in our debauchery, or so it seems. And I don't mean the tribes...I mean the Greeks. You've never seen anybody snobbier or prouder than that Egyptian crowd in your life."

"Have they started trading?"

"Not much. They've got some young prince with them, well-grown but haughty. Wouldn't even call on the leading citizens though they ran to him soon enough. All the world loves a prince. Especially a rich prince."

I'd seen too many royal knees a-tremble to be awed by any crowned heads. "I saw an Egyptian in the agora. He seemed very interested in me."

"Maybe that's why he's not calling on any of the Houses of Eros," she said, winking. The thick kohl seemed to stick together and she rubbed vigorously to get her eye opened again. She swung her feet to the floor.

"So, as I'm not on the menu, our mothers being cousins and all, what do you want? I've got a couple of nice bright girls in the house or you can wait 'til the best gets back. She sings too, so she's a favorite at parties. The chief oil merchant is entertaining tonight but they don't keep it up late so she'll be back before moonrise."

When I hesitated, she added, "It's on the house."

Well, it isn't polite to refuse true hospitality.

In the morning, after kissing a hung-over Petta farewell, I made my way to the Temple of Ares behind the marketplace. Some say the god of War came originally from Thrace, that his balls-out love of warfare is something he shares with the men of my land. All I know is that he was the first god I ever worshipped, though not under that name.

His veneration, along with supplications to the wind and the grass, were passed on father to son from time immemorial. I couldn't pass through Kalithanos without a visit to his temple, especially after Ares and I had met face-to-face some months earlier, when I'd alerted the gods to a danger they'd long forgotten. I was still sorting all the events of that time out in my mind as I gazed up at his idealized features.

Maybe that's why I didn't sense them until they were standing on either side of me.

"Mister Hebnetma wants to see you." He was the taller by a hair.

"Mister Hebnetma doesn't like to be kept waiting." The other one's shoulders were broader by a fingernail's width.

"Who's Mr. Hebnetma?" I asked.

"Hur, hur, hur," laughed Taller, from his belly.

"Tsh, tsh, tsh," Broader snickered through his wide white teeth.

In the dimness of the temple, their skin gleamed like well-tended armor, hammered into a perfection of muscle rarely achieved by men. But they weren't wearing armor or even tunics. They wore only pleated linen kilts that left their melon-sized knees bare. Their broad, pink-soled feet were equally naked. Each had a *wadjet*, the Eye of Horus, tattooed on both pectoral muscles, the dark ink hard to see against the color of their skin.

"He's not that Egyptian I saw in the marketplace? What does he want?"

"He didn't say," Taller admitted. "He said, 'bring him' and here we are. He wanted to see you yesterday."

In another second, they would put their hands on me and hustle me out. I have no objection to being touched in the way of business, fights and so on, but I don't like being man-handled.

I turned toward the door and started to walk out. "Aren't you coming?" I threw over my shoulder.

Outside, I encouraged them to walk ahead of me, "to show me the way." Broader kept trying to fall behind but my courtesy in insisting that he go first confused him. They had the drill down for escorting the unwilling visitor which made me wonder all the more about their employer.

I was also interested to note that the appearance of two exceptionally large, nearly naked Nubian guards caused no comment or overt glances from the people we passed. A few children gaped; that was all.

The house they took me to had no distinguishing features from the others in the street. Once inside, however, we were in Egypt.

I almost stepped in the pool of clear water in the entry. A few pottery frogs sat on the bottom, life-like among the painted reeds. Lotus-shaped lamps burned, illuminating wall-paintings of animal-headed goddesses, their long hands upraised in welcome. Somewhere in a room beyond the foyer, someone strummed a harp with an accompaniment of quickly tinkling bells.

Despite these signs of occupancy, the house breathed emptiness. No upper servant came to take over from the Brawny Brothers. As Taller and Broader escorted me into the interior, I saw crates corded for shipment, swathed statues reminding me of mummies, and covered baskets huddling with bumpy bags stuffed square.

Entering an interior room, lit with a skylight, Taller knelt on one knee while Broader whispered in the ear of the slim young man I'd glimpsed in the marketplace. The two girl musicians stopped playing on our entrance and stood motionless to one side. They were lovely, cream-colored creatures, naked but for fringed bands around their hips. Dancers, then, as well as players.

Hebnetma picked up the goblet on the table at his elbow. "You are Eno the Thracian." It wasn't a question. "My master and uncle, the High Priest of Amun, has been searching for you. Where have you been?"

"Your master is not mine," I answered. I didn't like to be scolded like an erring schoolboy by some stranger at least half a dozen years younger than me. "I owe no man an explanation of my movements."

"Not even those who would hire you?"

"Not even them."

Egyptians have the oldest and most advanced civilization in the world. When the rest of us were wondering what those flanged blobs on the ends of our arms were good for, they were building the Pyramids. They'd invented writing, music, and chairs. I'd never met one yet who didn't feel he had a lot to live up to.

This one was the same. From his failure to stand for a guest to his self-consciously graceful movements, he was telling me that I was nothing but a barbarian who might prove to be useful but with no claim on his courtesy. He probably consoled himself with the idea that I wouldn't know I'd been insulted. I knew...I just didn't care. Much.

"I'm on a journey that won't wait."

"Yet you had time to dally with that female."

I kept my temper. "My apologies to the High Priest of Amun and all that. But I'm not taking on any work at present."

"It is a simple task for one of your reputation. Of course, the reward for your efforts will be plenteous." He turned out his wrist.

I found Taller presenting me with an open casket, the length of his not-inconsiderable forearm, brimming with gold arm-cuffs and gleaming jewels. The smell of cedar wood arose from the box, the smell of wealth.

Glancing at Hebnetma, I weighed him up. Egyptian and rich...possibly some off-shoot of a noble or even of the Royal House. Petta had called him a prince. Maybe he couldn't help his sneer. He might have been born with it. Or maybe it was just the eye makeup.

I reached out and snapped closed the lid. "Sorry. It's impossible. Catch me in two weeks when I get back. If you're still here, that is."

"I have been recalled to Thebes," he said. It was the first crack in his mask of superiority. Whatever was calling him home pleased him so much he couldn't help sharing his news even with an uncouth hillman like me.

"I hope you have better weather than we did. There's a whi...."

"Thank you for your concern," Hebnetma said. "But we, naturally, will be traveling in an Egyptian ship."

It was news to me that the nationality of a boat affected the weather or whirlpools. I let it pass. There's no point in teasing people like Hebnetma. If they could laugh at themselves, there'd be nothing to tease them about.

"I can give you the names of a couple of other heroes, if it's any good to you. There's a fellow in Mennefer, Anum-Dejehuty. He's a worthy hero."

"Ah, yes, there was a note about him. Did you know him well?"

The past tense made me look at him hard. "Not really. Is he dead?"

"Alas, several of those my master has graced with his service are now serving Amun-Ra in the Field of Reeds."

"Several?" I shook my head, warning bells pinging all over me. "It's intriguing but I should be going. I have a long trip ahead of me."

His moral superiority suffered another crack when he unbent enough to ask the question that had been on his tongue since I came in. "What is so important that you will pass up a fortune?"

"I'm going to see my mother," I said and waited for the laugh.

Hebnetma stood up. "I honor you for your filial piety, Eno the Thracian. My own mother would never forgive me if I stayed your steps unnecessarily."

He walked over to me, the beads on his wig clacking together. Flipping open the box, he fished out a slender gold bangle, adorned with a single black onyx stone. It was inscribed with a highly detailed beetle, a symbol of long life. "A gift for the mother of so great a son."

At least it sounded like a compliment, though 'great' could just mean 'over-large'. I accepted with wary thanks. Gold is plentiful in Egypt, both the mineral and the beautiful wheat that is the second source of their wealth. If it had been a silver bangle, I would have refused it as being worth too much. Because of its comparative rarity, silver is often more prized among the Egyptians than gold.

Taller and Broader showed me out. As I passed the fountain in the foyer, I heard female voices.

Hoping for another glance at the dancing girls, I turned my head. But two other women stood there, one mature of face and figure. Her elaborate wig woven with golden beads didn't distract my eyes from the unhappy lines around her thin mouth.

The other one was young and fresh-faced, a flush of health on her high, round cheeks. Her dark eyes met mine and I nodded to her. The smile faded from her lips and she stared after me, as haughty as Hebnetma. There was a great resemblance between them, even more than just their pride. Mother and sister to the young man?

Taller opened the door. "I'm turned around," I said. "Which way to the marketplace?"

Broader pointed with his chin, his massive arms too valuable to be used unnecessarily. "That way."

"Thanks. If you're ever in Piraeus, look me up. Anyone can tell you where to find me."

I'd walked half a dozen steps when one of them called my name. I waited while he jogged up to me. It was like watching a living rock slide. "You were smart not to take the job," Taller murmured as he pretended to press a dropped object into my hand. "I've heard everyone they've hired has failed big time...as in last job ever."

"You know anything about it?"

"Only that we aren't going to be volunteering for anything when we get home."

"Truly is it said that wisdom is above rubies. Good luck to you."

"And to you also."

* * *

I turned my back on Kalithanos, taking the Northern Road. For the first mile or so, it was the same as any other place. A few noisome trash heaps, eager visitors from the sticks beside themselves with excitement at visiting the big town, and livestock belonging to the huts straggling out from the city limits. Sometimes all three collided, to the amusement of the locals.

But once beyond the last traces of town, the road ran straight. The groups that I saw were all coming toward me, some silent with weariness, some chattering with eagerness. I saw no one traveling alone and remembered my cousin's fears. Soon, the groups were farther apart and fewer yet.

As I traveled on, leaving the miles behind me, the air began to change.

Everywhere you go in Greece, or so it seems to me, you can smell the combination of salt, wet, and rotten fish that is the Sea. Bracing, certainly. People take deep breaths, expelling it with a lusty 'Ha!" and tell the world at large how good it is to be alive. I enjoy it myself and, on some bright mornings after an energetic swim, have even said 'Ha!"

As I pressed on into the countryside, leaving the sea-smell behind me, I realized it was the fragrance of dust, of pine, of ancient leaf-mold replenished autumn after autumn, that spoke to me of 'home.' Songs of my childhood returned to me as I strode along. Most of them, truthfully, were the bawdier ones that the men sang when the pungent liquor we brewed ourselves went around the fire. We young boys would listen through the cracks in our doorways, giggling at the few words we knew we weren't supposed to say in front of our parents.

The silence amplified my footsteps as I marked time to "The Shepherd's Last Shearing". The refrain is essentially 'baa, baa, baa.' I only stopped singing when it seemed like the sheep roaming the pastures alongside me were joining in a little too enthusiastically. Or maybe I just sang about as well as they did.

It was when I'd stopped to take a stone from my boot that I got that 'watched' feeling again. But I had not passed another mortal for a good span of the sun. I took a lot longer over the stone than it needed and eventually heard the slow clip-clop of a horse coming up the slight rise I'd just climbed. I drew back a little into the shade of a small cluster of trees near the top. I was just curious, not scenting any danger.

My curiosity ramped up when the rider came no further. Had he seen that the road was empty now? If so, what difference did it make to him?

We waited out of sight of each other until the birds overhead became so used to me standing there motionlessly that they started to sing again. I was pretty sure a spider had started spinning a web between the nearest tree and my neck.

Then I laughed. The rider likely thought I was lying in wait for him, a robber by the side of the road.

Not wanting to hang around all afternoon when I still had miles before me, I walked out, doing my best imitation of a traveler who'd done no more than ease nature out of sight of the road. Though an unusual delicacy in these parts, I hoped it would allay the rider's fears and allowed me to hail him. I didn't exactly mind no company except my own but maybe he'd prove to keep a new tale or two under his tongue.

I walked on, expecting every moment to hear hooves coming up behind me but there was nothing. Had I imagined it, conjuring the sound from the hunger of my ears? Or was he so wary that he assumed my re-appearance was just a ploy to draw him out? In which case, he was right though for the wrong reason. I couldn't very well turn around and swear I meant him no harm. Who would believe it?

When he still didn't appear, I dismissed him from my thoughts and walked on for another hour or so. The clouds were piling up above the growing mountains ahead of me. Though they were magnificent with the golden afternoon sunlight behind them, shading from purest white on the rippling peaks to increasingly dark grey in their valleys, they foretold rain and heavy rain at that.

I soon came to the point of decision. The road divided, branching off to the south-east, meeting at my feet with another way. This climbed up into the forests and rocks of the far Slipstone Pass. The southern road swung in a wide bend around the mountains, the grass trampled into dust by the shuffling of many heavily laden feet. A well stood in the fork, a good place to fill your waterskins and beasts before trekking farther on.

The mountain road had long grass growing over the track, thick enough to graze on. But it takes more than a season or two to smother all traces of a hard-trodden road.

Uncorking my wineskin, I sprinkled a good measure upon the ground near to the well. Perhaps the spirit of the well would like a spicy red wine. I was asking less for guidance than for wisdom.

If I headed south, I'd be at least ten days on the way. Over the pass, two or three days' travel at most, depending on the weather, would see me down the far side. Then one more day, a night, and perhaps half a day more to my old village.

I took a good swallow of the wine and started toward the mountain.

* * *

I stopped earlier than I'd originally planned. The clouds were growing darker, their swollen undersides ready to deliver. I chose a spot not far from a creek and tied my rope to two trees, stretched out to receive the oiled canvas I'd rolled up tightly and slung under the straps of my pack. A few rocks around the edges to keep them from flapping in the wind and my tent was snug from everything but biting gnats.

Kindling a small fire, I heated up the sausages I'd bought that morning and toasted the flat bread. The only thing I'd wished I'd bought was a small pot of pickle but I knew it would seem intolerably heavy and useless after a few days' walking.

The wind began to growl like a dog unsure if another dog were friend or foe. Then, far-off, thunder answered like a dog with no doubts at all.

I walked down to the creek to wash my hands and face. There was a clear space above my head. Looking up, I saw the tops of the trees bowing gracefully to a wind I could not yet feel on the ground. Lightning came, still far-off but capable of waking the thunder which rolled like great balls off the sides of the near-by hills. I prayed briefly that Zeus the Thunderer would enjoy his target practice but keep his bolts far from me.

My tent was flimsy, certainly, but it seemed like ideal shelter at the moment.

I hurried back, kicking dirt over my fire so the wind couldn't catch up a single spark and hurl it at my only refuge. Just as big drops began to make craters in the soft dust, I ducked into my tent.

A girl sat up, clutching a blanket to her bare chest. I recognized her as the girl I'd passed as I'd left Hebnetma's house. Her dark-rimmed eyes were huge in the dim light and she winced as the thunder punched the air. "Do you think my horse will be all right in the barn?"

I reeled out into the rain, half-wrecking the setup. I heard her squeak as the rain blew in, which was evidence that I wasn't dreaming or mad. Where had she come from? What was she doing here?

The big drops fell harder and faster. I ducked under the tent again. "What barn?"

"What?"

"You said something about a barn?"

She pointed over her bare shoulder. "A little farther up the road. A thousand cubits, no more."

Without looking at her, I grabbed my gear. I stripped the tent off the rope. I made a quick decision not to try to untie it though I knew the rain would make the knots swell. She yelped again as the rain came down harder, drenching her naked skin and I threw the tent-cloth around her, muffling her from neck to toes.

Swinging my bag onto my shoulder, I scooped her up.

"Which way?"

CHAPTER THREE

To call it a barn was to grossly insult all self-respecting barns everywhere. This was a shelter, barely, for sheep and their shepherds during the spring birthing rush. The first wall was constructed from boards planed by a drunken carpenter with a palsy, and the other two by his less talented brother. Despite the fourth side being open to the elements, the whole place still reeked of sheep shit, a smell I'd hoped to have left behind me with my boyhood. The girl's frightened horse added valuable contributions to the local manure stocks every time the lightning flashed.

I was already missing my tent.

"Who are you?" I asked, putting her on her feet. "And what are you doing out here alone?"

She reeled off a succession of syllables. I plucked a couple of god-names out of the crowd but, by-and-large, it was just sounds. Despite wearing my tent like my great-grandmother's winding sheet and looking like something the hungriest cat would leave in the gutter, she still gazed pityingly at me for my barbarian ways.

"I am Naunet," she said slowly and clearly, as to a child. "Beloved of Maat, Orderer of the World."

With a name like that, no wonder she held herself with such pride even under these circumstances.

"I'm Eno." Suddenly my name seemed awfully short. I toyed with the idea of adding 'Defender of Aphrodite, destroyer of incredible monsters, and three time all-Athenian winner of the 'Spicy Snails' cooking contest' but I didn't want to boast.

"Yes, I know you are," she said boldly. "That's why I followed you." She pursed pretty lips. The lightning flickered like fireflies. "I must say, you weren't difficult to find. You took no precautions against danger."

"Why did you follow me?"

"The Oracle said I must."

"What Oracle?"

"All of them." She tried to bring out a hand, presumably to count on her fingers, but the tent was none too secure. I reached out and grabbed the slack around her neck before the whole thing fell off.

"Do you have clothes?"

"Yes, here." She wriggled under the tent.

"Then put them on...." I turned my back.

"But the Oracle said that you were to be my lover."

She couldn't have been seventeen and innocent buds of promise, though charming, aren't really what I'm looking for in a woman. "Oracles get things wrong all the time. I heard the one at Delphi has started drinking again."

"Oh, I didn't talk to her. My mother wanted me only to hear the words of the Egyptian gods. But they were very clear. Abydos, Kebet...I even ate the sacred lettuce and I hate that...and of course, I asked at the temple of the Great Sphinx. They all said the same thing."

I could hear rustling clearly over the hissing sound of the rain and a few delicate clinks and clanks. "All is well, turn again," she said.

Turning, I saw that Naunet wore, not the sheer linen of her nation, but the dress of a hill-woman, thickly-woven wool cloth much more suited to riding rough. Nevertheless true to her nature, she also wore half-a-dozen clanking bangles, a golden collar featuring a medallion with the Eye, and swaying earrings like little bells. She'd combed her hair too. While still wet, it no longer broke into ends and tentacles. She tilted her head like a sleepy kitten, inviting me to admire her.

"At least you won't catch your death of cold."

She pouted. It was cute, but still a pout. "Do you not want to know what the Oracles said?" she asked after a minute.

"You're really Queen of Upper and Lower Egypt and I'm the evil barbarian who has stolen you away, leaving your one true love to rescue you and dispatch me in a suitably gory ending?"

She laughed. I confess I'm susceptible to women's laughter. I always have a sneaking suspicion they're laughing at me anyway, so I try to make them at least smile.

"No. They said that I would meet a strong barbarian from the North who would rescue me from deadly peril and...."

"And..." I prompted her, kicking myself for it.

"And that's when it got confusing. I...I don't know the right word."

"Your Greek is very good," I said.

"Thank you. My governess is a Greek, from Athens. Her father was a great thinker. A genius."

"We are oversupplied with those."

"What does that mean?"

"Never mind. You have been well-taught."

She ducked her head in a graceful acknowledgement. Then she shifted uncomfortably. "I wish to sit down," she said.

I'd noticed a half-rotten feeding trough in the dimness. I picked it up and flipped it over, wiping away the top layer of moss and little insects with the edge of my hand. "Sit here. Or on the horse."

Naunet showed no signs of fastidiousness. "You are very resourceful."

"Are you hungry? I could start a fire and toast some sausages."

"Oh, no, thank you. My mother packed me a very nice dinner. I ate it all."

"Your mother? She knows about this little adventure?"

"Oh, yes. She sent me, upon the Oracle's words. But I would not call this an adventure. Rain? A little dirt? Nothing. These are not deadly perils."

I ran a hand over my short-cropped hair, removing the last of the rainwater, though I felt it mist up again in an instant. "I think a fire would be a useful thing right now." I didn't want to insult her by insinuating that she was turning blue from cold, so I added a quick excuse. "It'll keep the bears off."

"Bears?" She rolled the word around her mouth. "What are 'bears', please?"

"Like a lion, but they walk sometimes on their hind legs. Big paws, big claws."

"Lions that walk upright? I should like to see that." She would have used to same disbelieving tone if I'd told her I'd talked to the gods face-to-face and that was as true as the other.

I wondered who had sheltered her from the bear-baiting that went on in towns like Kalithanos. They hadn't seemed to bother sheltering her from much else. Girls weren't like this in the Greek city-states. You hardly ever saw one once they'd passed childhood. They lived in the inner courts of their homes, spinning, weaving, teaching their siblings or their children. Only on the great festival days did they emerge, like butterflies, to spend a few short hours in praise of Demeter or Artemis or Hera, then they'd return to their trammeled life. I suppose they don't mind it, not that they had a great deal of choice in the matter.

Among my people, the women work as hard, and certainly longer, than the men. They are up before us, churning butter from the cows they've milked before sunrise, making food, washing children, plaiting ropes, scraping hides, and always cleaning. We men yawn, stretch, and scratch before eating the food, tousling the children, spilling the butter from the churn-bag, and leaving our big footprints in the carefully swept dirt. Mothers are usually hard-pressed to hide their pleasure when their sons go out to spend the long summer months in higher pastures with their sheep and goats. I will say mine was always glad to see me again when the nights grew longer and I returned.

"It is impossible to make a fire, anyway," Naunet said. "It is too wet. It has rained, and rained, and rained for days. We do not have such times in Egypt."

"Nor such grass."

"Our grass is very good. I will not say 'better' as this is your country and my brother tells me I should not be rude."

"Hebnetma is your brother?"

"Yes." Naunet didn't seem to want to add to that, though it didn't take an oracle to understand she was not pleased with him.

"It looked like you were packing up to go home."

"Yes." Then she smiled. "This is why I am following you. I cannot go home without you. For how can I know when the deadly peril will find me? It might be a sea-monster, or a shipwreck, or an evil spirit."

She was cute but not cute enough to tempt me from my path. "I'm going to my village," I said, using no fancy words. "I want to see someone there. It's going to take me a week to walk it and then I'm hoping to stay with her for a few weeks. I haven't seen her in...." I reflected but could not recall quite how long it had been, which told its own tale. "In a long time."

"Your wife? She will have taken another husband by now. A sweetheart? She will be married or dead. You should not waste time on such women when you have me."

"Naunet, it's my mother."

"Oh. Then you must go. I will go with you. She will like to meet me."

I have met starving ticks with less desire to attach themselves to me.

She hurried to reassure me. "You need not worry. I know just how to act around her. I will be sweet as a honey-cake, never argue with her and praise you often. She will not think I am good enough for you, but she will agree to our being together. Do we leave at first light?"

"Yes. You leave to go down the mountain and I leave to go up the mountain."

I thought about my cousin's warning. Maybe I could accompany her back to the fork in the road, find an old woman going back to Kalithanos to shepherd her. A few coins should be persuasion enough for anyone.

"Don't be silly." She shivered. "If you are going to light a fire, do so."

I could continue to develop my calluses by using my fire-bow and soft wood shreds to start a new flame. Or I could act like a man and dash back to my first fire to see if any coals had survived the dirt and the rain. The second seemed easiest.

I hate to admit it but I got lost. I know...I know. Hero. Smarter, stronger, braver. And just as lost in the dark and the wet as any wide-eyed cub straying from the cave for the first time.

I don't know how long I stumbled around, tripping over roots, getting damper and more furious with myself as the seconds passed. I have known some miserable nights on bivouac when the sand-fleas danced the saraband on my body or when a foot-fungus grew so rapidly you could watch it conquer new territory faster than the army ever did. But that night in my own homeland was as miserable as they were in its own unique way.

I thanked the gods individually and collectively when I glimpsed the fire. It wasn't the one I'd extinguished, returned to life by some miracle. This one burned merrily in the mouth of a half tumbled-down barn, that sheltered a frightened, incontinent horse and a liquid-eyed Egyptian girl.

I bowed before her and rendered my heart-felt thanks for the warmth and light and guidance in passable Court Egyptian. Those black eyes widened. "Very good," she said, clapping her hands. "You did not tell me you spoke my language."

In Greece, a citizen of Argos can make himself easily understood in Lemnos, though most of the Archipelago Sea lies between. There may be differences in a word here or there or a pronunciation but a little good-will smooths over all such bumps.

In Egypt, one end of the Nile cannot understand the other and anything you say isn't too comprehensible in any of the towns along the way.

They even say that gibberish sounds like a man from the Delta trying to arrange friendly relations with a woman from Elephantine.

Fortunately, Noble or Court Egyptian, being very ancient and largely unchanged, is understood throughout the Nile-lands, Upper and Lower. It is also almost completely free of modern words like *octopus*, *bathtub*, or *independent contractor*. This made ordinary commerce difficult, especially as it pertains to me. The closest it could come to *freeman*, for instance, was *someone else's slave*.

I spread out my hands to the fire. "How did you do it?"

She showed me the cleverly made double-walled pot with the replenished coal inside. "In case it gets too hot on the outside, we keep it in this little mud basket which we keep damp."

"Civilization," I said. "You can't beat it."

Dry goat dung makes excellent fuel, if smelly. I wouldn't have cared to cook over it now, though I don't think I was so fussy in my childhood. Nevertheless, the friendly glow warmed more than the meager shelter. Even the horse seemed comforted.

Naunet had made herself useful in my absence, managing to kick or sweep a clearer spot on the floor to spread out my ground cloth and to rig the tent between us and the rain coming in at the back. This fell down about as often as it stayed up. She'd make a sound like a spitting kitten and fix it again.

"You must be tired," I said, wiping the rainwater off my arms.

"Oh, no." She tried to look bright but her heavy eyes belied her attempt to sound cheerful and quite, quite awake. I doubted she'd ever spent as much as an hour all together in the saddle in her life.

Realizing that lead me to know there was no way she'd be able to ride back to town tomorrow. She'd be lucky to stand without pain.

"Tell me what else those oracles said," I asked, sitting down.

Naunet knelt with perfect poise, her clasped hands to her chest, her eyes sparkling. "As I said, we are to be..."

"Wait. Why did you go to an oracle in the first place? Is it traditional for a young girl to do so? Say before she is married?"

"Oh, no. It is too expensive, though the One Who Praises Min did not charge us. He only asked that I remember the Old god in the days of my prosperity." She giggled in reminiscence. "Mother said that the gods had better give us prosperity soon if they expect to get anything back."

"You don't seem to be suffering from poverty." I looked at her jewelry.

"Oh, trinkets," she said scornfully. "Faience and paint."

"But nice faience and paint. Very realistic."

Nobody fakes the look of gems like an Egyptian craftsman. Our kings don't wear jewels much but our queens make up for it. And when you've got wars and famines and other expenses of statecraft, adorning her majesty with fake jewels impresses bankers just as much as the real stuff. No one's going to get close enough to examine those rubies and emeralds.

"You'll like my mother," Naunet said. "She's had a disappointing life but she always makes us laugh. Why, once...."

I listened to long story about a fish and a foolish servant but Naunet kept forgetting the Greek for various household items and I lost the point of the joke. I chuckled politely when it seemed called for.

"The oracle?" I prompted. She'd been fast enough with part of the prophecy. What wasn't she saying?

"My uncle, the High Priest of Amun, suggested we see his oracle when it all started happening. He sent us to the one at Abydos because he thought it was woman's problem. It was in my bedroom, after all. She was the first one to mention you but Mother didn't think a barbarian would be much use...." She clapped her hand to her mouth and looked over it at me with stricken eyes.

"She's probably right about that," I said, my heart unwrung.

"Of course she changed her mind when the next oracle said the same thing. And the one after that."

"And that is...?" I prompted.

"That we are to be lovers, that you will save me from deadly peril and that you will send this ghost to rest in his tomb. I do not know if the ghost is the deadly peril or not but Mother is afraid that it may be. That is why we came with my brother to Kalithanos, though it is not usual for women to come on official business."

"A ghost. Whose ghost?" I found that if I concentrated I could follow the gist of her story without getting sidetracked by the digressions that decorated her conversations.

"I do not know. No one can tell me that, though I think the One Who Praises Min may have guessed. But you know what oracles are like."

She peeped at me with her big brown eyes, judging whether I believed her or not. I kept my face very still, as I gazed into the heart of the fire. "What happened, exactly?"

"A ghost, wandering through my chamber. It stands at the end of my sleeping mat and moans. Sometimes it paces back and forth, sometimes it just stands there and stares at me."

"You tried moving to another room?"

"Of course. But it always finds me. Even when we were traveling around to the shrines. And...." She sighed.

"We went on a visit to the family of Baruti-Kosey, my...my...our fathers had arranged long ago that our families would unite. I prayed to the Great Mother and to Amun that the ghost would not follow me there. But it did. They have sent back our gifts, even the linen I worked myself. And the stories started to go around...." She sighed again, then broke out with, "Really, you don't know how untidy a ghost makes a girl feel. As if her skirt were dirty in the back...if you understand me?"

I wouldn't have put it just like that but I knew what she meant. I had a few ghosts of my own. Mine didn't stalk around my bedroom at night, moaning. Mine lived in my head and could be heard by day or night if I let them speak. I'd gotten good at shutting them up but they were sly. I'd be walking along, happy as a puppy with an old rope, then the past would rise and walk with me.

"We all have ghosts," I said. "It's part of surviving."

"What have I survived?" she demanded. "Nothing. No one can say 'Naunet has hurt me, Naunet is my enemy.' If I were to pass to Osiris tonight, my heart would not sway the balance scales against the feather of truth."

"We'll hope it won't come to that."

I thought about her problem. "Did the ghost follow you to Kalithanos?"

"I have not seen him since we stepped foot on the ship that brought us hither."

"Problem solved then. Don't go back to Egypt."

She blinked those depthless eyes once, twice. "Not go back?" Then Naunet laughed for obviously I must have been joking.

The rain had slowed until I couldn't tell if it now fell from the sky or merely dripped off the leaves. Thunder sounded far off, like a pot falling down a flight of stairs in a neighboring house. "You should get some sleep," I said. "You'll go back down the mountain in the morning."

"But...."

I held up my hand. "No arguing. You shouldn't have come. I have to go on up to my village and it's a hard path."

Naunet nodded. "It is too late to argue now. Sleep will not stay off the back of my neck." My expression must have shown my confusion. She laughed and demonstrated the meaning of this saying, her head falling forward as limp as boiled celery.

I stayed awake while she turned round and round like a cat looking for a soft spot in the middle of a sleeper's stomach. She wished me a pleasant night or so I assumed, her voice soft but with a merry laugh in the depths. I wondered if my Egyptian was good enough to persuade her to go home the next day.

I poked some more dry dung on the fire and sat watching the flames. The trees looked very black and wet beyond the orange light. We had been both envious and contemptuous, my friends and I, of the people who lived in the softer lands we could see from our hillsides. They had wide fields to till while we clung precariously, one leg longer than the other, to the tiny patches of flat land capable of holding a thimble of soil and a fast-rooting crop. We wondered aloud how the valley dwellers had borne seeing so little of the sky between their trees. And Marbi had never tired of telling us of the vileness of some fishy potion a traveling medicine man had given him when his father had taken him down into the dirty little town whose smoke we could see. That potion had probably saved his life when he'd been deathly sick with a fever but it wouldn't have been fair for any of us to admit it.

I'd been so concentrated on seeing my mother that I'd forgotten I'd see Marbi and Thumbless (so-called for his clumsy ways than for any physical lack) and Bron again, if none of them had departed for the Underworld. Though my profession demanded I meet risks most people would never know, from fighting carnivorous geese to wrestling in thought with crafty viziers in secret mountain hideaways, I knew that more men died from a scratch gone bad or their wife's cooking than ever died in combat.

I sent a prayer up that each of my boyhood friends were as hale as I myself. I must have nodded off for they came and stood around me, no older than they'd been the last time I'd seen them. Bron smiled down at me. Thumbless and Marbi shook their shaggy heads. "He's grown," one said.

"Older but not wiser."

"Always knew he'd come to a bad end."

If it hadn't been a dream, one or more of us would have wound up with our heads in a rain barrel. All our quarrels ended like that, with laughter and somebody shaking the water out of his eyes. Or brushing the dirt off his head, if there'd been no rain.

"That's what you get for letting a girl tag along," Marbi said.

"He can't help it if he's too dumb to stay awake."

"Hey..." I said. "That's enough."

"Enough. You used to be first, now you've got to follow. Trouble, nothing but trouble."

They'd begun to fade; I could see the bright firelight through them. Only it didn't look right. I could see that the flames were nearly out, only smoldering logs hatchmarked from burning, and even as I looked the last whole one crumbled, eaten away underneath. But the light did not grow less.

I snapped awake, realizing that the streaming orange light was the dawn.

Naturally, the girl was gone. Had she been a dream too? The evidence her horse had left behind broke that theory into pieces. Perhaps she'd been smart and gone back to Kalithanos. Somehow, though, I doubted it. Again I remembered Petta's warning.

"Ghosts...demons...ill-luck." Ghosts, Naunet could maybe handle. She'd need me for the others.

CHAPTER FOUR

I tracked her by the mud her horse's hooves had stirred up. Not surprisingly, the tracks ran up into the hills.

With a sigh that came from my boots, I started after her. At this rate, she'd be lucky if the 'deadly peril' she escaped wasn't me.

Everything was dripping. Deep ruts ran along the road where the main rush of water had run. The ground steamed. The air was thick, heavy with the smell of rich rot.

I kept to the high apex in the middle of the road. The hoof prints were there as well, close together, showing me that Naunet had the sense to go slow. A misstep could pitch her over the edge where there was nothing to break her fall except the river far away at the bottom.

There were no other footprints. No one besides Naunet had passed that way but that didn't mean she wouldn't meet with trouble. A girl alone was fair game even, or especially, in the heart of a great city let alone on a deserted hillside. Naunet's exotic elegance might tempt any man and some of these mountain types weren't fussy at the best of times. Any girl who didn't smell like a goat would have suitors a-plenty.

I started to jog. I couldn't beat a running horse, but I could catch up to an ambling one, provided I didn't fall off the cliff either.

I ran right past the old woman resting on a large boulder, nestled among the trees. Backing up, I greeted her. "Good morning, Grandmother."

She blinked up at me. Her face was seamed with a thousand wrinkles, clustering about her eyes and breaking away down her cheeks. But the eyes in their tangle of lines were bright and sharp as a hungry bird's.

In answer to my greeting, she only grunted. I tried again in one of the more common dialects.

"Good morning, good morning," she answered in Greek that creaked like a rusty chain. "Do I have nothing to do but greet foolish travelers?" She spat past my foot.

"Did you happen to see a girl on a horse pass this way?"

"And you with your eyes on the ground? What do you think?"

I thought it was odd that this crusty old woman had left no tracks herself in the mud. I shot a glance at her feet but they were out of sight beneath the clean hem of her black robe.

Now it would be fair to say that I have more experience than most men with the gods and their ways. One thing I have learned is that they really only have one joke.

Men laugh at many things, from 'A centaur and a sphinx walk into a taverna...' to a sad-faced clown chasing a dog running away with a sausage. I'm partial to a good mimic myself. The gods, however, seem to find humor only in pretending to be human. Thus have many entertained them unaware, except for the consequences which may be hilarious to the god in question but tends to end short and sharp for the mortal. Maybe that's the best part of the joke.

The ragged stranger who happens to drop a pair of winged sandals. The lovely girl who offers good advice on how to dispatch a monster. The old woman sitting by the side of the road?

"Have you come far today, Grandmother?"

"Very far. Any distance seems long when you are alone."

"True. That's why I'm looking for the girl."

She chuckled or choked on phlegm. It was hard to tell. "I saw her," she admitted. "Pretty little thing. Dazzled these old eyes."

I recalled another crone I'd met who turned out to be the Goddess of Love herself in disguise. I suppose if you could look like anything or anyone, you'd get a certain amount of entertainment out of it. Of course, the mortal couldn't come right out and ask. Whispering to some old beldame, 'you're really Aphrodite, aren't you?' would either get my face slapped, give me a romantic relationship I seriously didn't want, or, worst of all, make the real goddess mad at me. I'd seen the Beauteous One slightly ticked off at one time. I never wanted to see her or any other of the Olympians in a full-on rage. Of all possible futures, being blasted into a molten puddle held the least attraction for me.

"So...you saw the girl."

"Her shadow passed over me. I was minded to ask her for a ride on that fine horse. Me old legs...." She coughed richly. "Me old legs failed as I come up the hill." She hooked a crooked thumb back at the densely wooded land behind her.

"Why didn't you use the road?"

"I has my secret ways," she said, possibly winking. "Oh, dearie! Me poor, poor legs."

I tried valiantly to hide my sigh. "Where are you going to, Grandmother?"

"I be bringing a little gift for my sisters who dwell atop this mountain." She glanced at the small bundle at the base of the rock. It was all wrapped up in linen so old it had gone gray, but from the shape it looked like a covered basket, longer than it was wide and with rounded ends.

"Shall I carry it for you?" I was going that way and it couldn't slow me down much.

"Such a nice boy...."

I wound up with the old woman on my back, my gear a cushion for her. Under all the robes, she was as thin and tough as a vine. Her knees gripped my kidneys and her fingers dug into my shoulders. Her bundle seemed all awkward corners and no grip I tried kept it from bumping and bruising me. It was also surprisingly heavy for its size.

The road did not improve as it wound its way around the mountain. The drop from the right side drew steadily deeper even as the road grew more narrow. I could still see Naunet's trail ahead, though the tracks looked a little smeared. Sometimes there were freshets running white and foaming off the mountain, the collected waters from last night's rain. I had to jump over the wider ones. The old woman on my back would give a gasp and her grip on me grew a little tighter. After a few of these, I noticed that her grasp did not relax once the jump was over.

She began to sing after a short while, a whispering song in a language I did not know. If she'd sung out, maybe I wouldn't have minded so much but the sibilant whispering was just on the edge of hearing, like listening to people talking in another room. I could neither make out a meaning nor shut my ears. The rhythm was almost impossible to walk to and the tune seemed to twine in my head, interrupting my thoughts.

"What's that song?"

"Oh, 'tis old, very old. Our mother taught it to us, long, long ago."

Her hands seemed to be growing colder. For an old bag of bones, she was getting heavier by the step, but surely I threw around more weight than her every day at the gymnasium.

I stumbled and the side of the mountain was very near. The old woman drew breath in a hiss.

"Careful!"

"Are you slipping?"

"No, but be careful."

Vaguely at the back of my mind, I knew something was wrong. But all I could hear was that whispering tune, never keeping to the same key, wandering high and low almost without pattern, forcing me to pay attention to catch the changes. My thoughts were marshaled into line like well-trained troops.

I whistled along and wondered why I'd thought it strange. My steps swung to the beat of that easy cadence and I decided it was worth listening even more closely. Perhaps I could learn it, if I paid enough attention.

"What's it called, Grandmother?"

"We call it the bridle song."

"Oh? Does it work on horses?"

"Some mounts respond better than others. Walk a little faster; I don't have all day." She began to sing again, louder but no more clearly. I couldn't understand the words any better though I recognized the sound of a few when they were repeated. I began to wait for those sounds, and hardly noticed that I was climbing very high. The road had become steep, so that sometimes I had to use my hands to keep from falling.

The bony knees that had dug into my sides were now crossed around my middle like a belt. Her chin, sharp and hard as a flint, dug into the hollow of my shoulder bones. The hands that had ridden on my shoulders now clutched each other tightly, her arms encircling my wide chest. She'd been so little sitting by the road. How was she now stretching her limbs so far?

In idle curiosity, I glanced down at the all-but fleshless hands and stringy arms. The once-hidden feet crossed beneath my belly and they glistened with scales, silver-green in the sunlight. There were no toes, only a scalloped edge where a web like an arch spread from side to side. I didn't dare turn my head to see what manner of face might be resting so close to my own...or what teeth it had.

The knowledge that something horrible had me in so intimate and strong a grip snapped the spell of her song. I wondered if she would know she no longer had control or if I could fool her. Well, at least I had the satisfaction, possibly short-lived, of knowing what the trouble was at Slipstone Pass at the top of the Black Mountain.

"Dry country, this," I said. "Do you know of a spring where I might drink?"

"Plenty to drink at my sisters' house. Plenty to eat there, too. There's my gift but you will make it look paltry indeed. Still we can save it for dessert." Her breath was ghastly foul but oddly familiar. Where had I met that stench of decay and blood before? It had something to do with this land, my beautiful native land.

There were plenty of monsters roaming the landscape in Thrace as our parents had told us when we were naughty or tempted to wander from our sheep. The motherly ghost so kind and tender to good children but who snatches bad children away to the bottom of a lake or the little spirits who held up lights to tempt away forever any child who got out of bed at night had been favorites of my own mother. Those were the mild ones, compared to what goaded older brothers and fed-up sisters would tell. But no one, so far as I knew, had a tale about an old woman who lured travelers into carrying her and then found it impossible to put her down again. She must be new, I thought, and no ornament to the landscape.

She didn't sing anymore but she hummed, a buzzing sound like a trapped fly.

"That tickles my ear, Grandmother."

"Does it, now?" Her voice had thickened, the already-mumbled words forcing themselves out through the gods knew what kind of teeth and jaw.

"Is it very much farther?" I asked, trying for the tone of a sleepy but patient child without overdoing it.

"Turn here," she said. "And you'll soon have a nice long sleep...."

A narrow off-shoot of the road turned to the left. It was little more than a worn-away line among the leaf-mold under the trees; I would have passed it by without a thought if it hadn't been for Naunet's tracks turning that way.

Sure enough, the first thing I saw at the end of the track was Naunet's horse. It stood against the outer wall of a cave and was shivering all over in long shudders, its head hanging down. Foam dripped from its jaws.

I didn't see Naunet.

At the same moment, I remembered where I'd met that foul breath of the hag before. When I was a boy, on another mountain not far from here, there'd been a family of cannibals. Their whole filthy camp had reeked of that gagging stench. But they, at least, had been recognizably human.

This hag was something else again. And where were her 'sisters'? I prayed they had not started the feast early, with Naunet as a dainty precursor to a more substantial meal, namely...me.

The one on my back gave forth a wheedling cry, in a voice more like a bird's than a woman's. An answering cry came from within the cave. It was not a large airy opening, but a narrow slit in the side of the rocks. A dreadful flopping, thumping sound came from the cave, followed by two enchanting voices, youthful, expressive, and sweet as flutes.

"Don't push!"

"Don't shove! Look out, you'll have me over in a minute!"

"Serves you right. I'm the oldest; I should go first."

"I'm the youngest; I should go first."

The one on my back gave a resigned sigh through her teeth. It sounded exactly like my own oldest sister's exasperation when my brother and I would fuss at each other.

"Come see what I've brought! Presents!"

"Put down the basket, fool," she said to me in a tone of command. I responded slowly, as if still rapt by the song she'd sung.

"Presents for you both! Such a feast as we've never known!" my passenger called again.

"Oh! Hurry up!"

"You stepped on my foot!"

"Well, get it out of my way, then, or I'll step on it harder next time!"

"I'll give you such a smack that your eye will fall right out of your face!"

Out they came, still pushing and shoving despite the wider space to stand in. They were as long and stringy as their sister, but one had only one large leg and foot which explained the thumping sound, and the other had only one eye, two legs, and about three times the arms most people found necessary. The arms were boneless as tentacles and moved with terrible speed and an almost complete lack of direction, flailing against each other.

Except for a bit of a pot-belly on the single-legged one, they were all three as skinny as cats' tails.

"Oooh," they said in unison, their voices riding a sliding scale, and started toward me, their sharp fingers outstretched.

The tentacled-one had two hands as well, terribly twisted, but still strong. They spread out on my chest, fingers cold and clammy, nails black as spears with dirt. Their long faces, with extended jaws and small sharp teeth, lifted to mine, sniffing and salivating. I tried not to recoil, to stay loose as if still under the spell.

"Pretty ladies...." I said dreamily.

The one clinging to my back laughed. "Get away! I get first choice."

They obeyed her, falling back, hungry hands supplicating. "But we're starving now! Just a little taste...."

I hoped again that Naunet was all right. Surely if they'd had anything to do with her, they would not now be so ravenous. But who could tell how often or how much such creatures needed to feed?

"Don't be greedy, my dears. This one will last us for weeks and weeks, fresh! Salt down the rest for the winter so he doesn't spoil, eh?"

The single-legged one leaped up and down, her powerful trunk giving her considerable bounce, her flat breasts flapping. "I've made a lovely egg and sumac sauce for the girl you sent. She's a sweet little morsel that will fry up light and fluffy for dessert. But this one..." She poked me in the ribs, rather rudely. "Hmmm, will take a lot of stewing to soften this cut. Too many muscles."

"Don't be so picky!" Miss Many-Arms said, giving her a nudge. "Boiled, fried, stewed or pickled, there's plenty here for all of us. You've done well, sister."

Their voices were so enchanting, full of good humor and lilting music, that it was easy to overlook the utter horror of what they were discussing. I could almost forget that I was the main course in this feast. I was even a little curious as to what sauce they would choose in the end. Had they ever considered capers and a little sweet onion, compounded with basil and marjoram? I almost wished I was not supposed to be under a spell so I could make the suggestion.

"You said I could have a sleep," I said complainingly, reminded of the role I was playing.

"So you shall, my little roast beef!" My passenger unwrapped her legs from around my waist, preparing to get down.

I widened my chest to its fullest, drawing in a vast breath. As if yawning, I raised my arms above my head, then, quick as a snap, I grabbed the hag by the nape of the neck and threw her forward over my shoulder.

She screamed as she hurtled down before me. I drew my sword as her two sisters flew at me, shrieking, tentacles and hands flailing, reaching out to strangle and claw. Their faces distorted even further with hatred and hunger, they snarled and bit toward me, their teeth clicking.

A tentacle, flung out at random, coiled about my neck. A burning necklace ringed my throat, as though acid dripped from every sucker.

I cut the single-footed one's head off and, with the return stroke, dispatched the other as well. Her tentacles lashed horribly for a moment even after her head shot off into the trees. They dropped like heavy sacks to the ground.

The tentacle around my neck dragged me forward. I sliced through it, then picked off the remains. The burning stayed behind, eating into my skin. I snatched up a handful of dirt and pressed it into the wound, dulling the pain as it neutralized the acid.

My passenger, the last one alive, scrambled backwards on her long limbs. They turned at strange angles, as though elbows and knees would bend in any direction.

I advanced on her, kicking the basket and the single-limbed one's head out of my way.

Tears, white and thick, came from her elongated eyes as she blinked triple lids. "You killed them! My sisters!"

"Yes. Now it's your turn."

"Wait! Stay your hand, fearsome warrior! Don't kill me. I will tell you all that you wish to know. All the answers to the questions you have about yourself...your father. Why journey to your mother's home? She will only lie to you."

"How do you know what I seek?"

She came upright, not by clinging to tree or wall, but by each limb twisting and clicking into place. "I can read you, Eno of the Maedi. My powers of prophesy come from our mother, a Siren from the Southern Sea. The others...." She looked past me at the corpses of her sisters. "They did not have it. They were fools; but I shall miss them."

She ground a palm against her face, wiping away the tears and snot. Her breath was coming fast, stirring the black rags she wore. "Will you spare my life, Eno, if I swear most faithfully to tell you all?"

"You know that cannibalism is the one crime the gods do not forgive. I cannot spare you for they would curse me with your punishment."

"Punishment? What worse punishment can they give me than this hideous form? You have killed my sisters. You will leave me to starve. Why shouldn't I tell your future? It is...."

A thud sounded, dull as a cracked bell. Suddenly her eyes rolled up in her head, showing the white. Her knees failed all directions at once as she sank to the ground at my feet.

Behind her was Naunet, tangled, bruised, torn, with a very large rock clutched in her hands. A greenish smear colored it. "That's enough of that," she said, in a housewifely tone.

The rock tumbled from her fingers as she swayed in a faint. I caught her up before she could fall and hurt herself or touch the thing she'd so neatly killed. I carried her to the horse, still shivering with terror but the only comfort in this cold camp.

Naunet was awake but dazed before I got her on the saddle. I uncorked my wineskin and held it to her lips. She took a sip, then a healthy swallow.

"Oh, I did it," she said, and put a delicate if dirty hand to her lips. "I killed her."

"Yes," I said, "You did."

"Are you angry? You didn't want to hear what it was going to say, did you?"

"I was...curious."

"No, you must not be. Not for the lies she would tell you out of hatred. She would twist everything. But everything!"

"You're probably right. She had little reason to tell me the truth." I looked up at the girl. "But what about you? What happened?"

"They called to me from the woods. One said the other had fallen into a pit and needed the horse to pull her out. I could not refuse such a request."

"I suppose not."

"Then they brought me here, tied me up and pushed me into the cave." She closed her eyes and a long shudder ran through her body as though she were about to be sick. "It's horrible in there. They...they cook."

"You're all right, though. They didn't hurt you?"

"I'm all right but it will be a long time before I visit another kitchen!"

CHAPTER FIVE

Naunet slid off the back of the horse and stamped her feet on the ground as if to test it and her own solidity. "Oh, poor horse," she said in quick sympathy. "You must have been terrified that they'd eat you first!"

It rolled a brown eye and lifted its head. Naunet patted the arched, sweating neck. "No one is going to eat you now. Or us either."

She looked up at me. "That was their intention?"

I nodded and she spat to one side. "What did you say about the gods? I couldn't hear your voice as clearly as...that other."

"Cannibalism is the only crime they can never condone. I think it goes back to their earliest beginning, when their own divine Father swallowed them whole. His name was Kronos and he is as fearsome and all devouring as Time and Chaos itself."

"You speak so confidently."

"I have reason to know. Anyway, then, Tantalus served them his own son to test their perception and he has suffered endless torment in the Underworld ever since."

"Well, so I should think! It was a stupid thing to do. A man should cherish his heir for it is he who will keep his father's spirit happy and fed in the Fields Eternal. No son means a starving ghost."

"Maybe that's why you have your ghost?"

She shook her head, the glossy black braids now adorning her head flying around her ears. "No, we tried taking new gifts to the family tomb as well. It made no difference. Oh, what's that?"

She leaped over the bodies of the monsters as blithely as though they were no more than fallen logs. Picking up the 'present', she shook it questioningly with her ear inclining toward it.

I followed with less grace, keeping a watchful eye on them. Plenty of monsters could regenerate or spawn into something worse. One of the little joys of my job.

Thinking over what I'd heard from my former passenger, I said, "I wouldn't open that...."

But Naunet had already whipped off the covering and lifted the latch. She peeped in and looked around at me with an expression of mingled pity and disgust wrinkling her smooth brow. "Oh, it's dead."

She put the basket down as gently as though the thing inside could still feel a jar.

Remembering the weight of it, I asked, "What is it? A dog?"

"No, a baby."

"What?"

I came closer and looked down. It seemed to sleep, pale and translucent as the wax effigies used in religious rituals. The golden lashes shaded the plump cheeks and it had perfect fingers and toes.

I put my hand on Naunet's shoulders. "We will bury it apart from these monsters."

She nodded. "I think we should burn them. We should not poison the earth with their rotting flesh."

Trust an Egyptian to see the practical side of death.

"I suppose," she said, "that you and I were just a lucky find. This poor mite must have been the meal they were planning."

"Not much for the three of them." I was reviewing all I knew of cannibals and their ways.

They liked their human nice and fresh. Dead meat wasn't usually to their liking.

"At least we can take it out..." She reached in and lifted it as though it were a living child, one hand under the head, the other supporting the napkin-wrapped seat.

Then she dropped it when it moved in her hands and cried.

I dove to my knees and made the cleverest catch of my life.

I rose up, trying to get a secure hold. The baby paused an instant, drew a big breath, and started crying again so loudly I felt trepanned. "Quick, put it back in the basket!"

"Don't be silly," Naunet said, taking it from me. "It's a good little baby." She began to rock it back and forth in a rhythm as old as time.

The basket looked ordinary enough. Made of plain willow twigs, stripped until flat, it formed a long oval. The handles turned on wooden pivots to leave the wooden top free to open on the side leather hinge. The thong that held it closed slipped over a small piece of white crystal, made dull by the many inclusions and cracks that ran through it. A few tattered ribbons in different colors, now faded, wound through the woven withes.

I put my hand in. It instantly felt as though I'd been sleeping on it all night. I tried to move it, even one finger, but everything from wrist to fingertip was numb. I drew it out quickly, knowing I'd been foolhardy, especially as it was my sword hand.

Just like the baby, it came almost immediately back to life. The tingles and prickles surged, somewhere between pain and tickling. Small wonder the kid had cried.

"Well, this would solve the problem of keeping meat fresh on long journeys." I realized a moment after I'd spoken that that was exactly what the hags had been using it for.

"I think that it is an abomination," Naunet said, using the Egyptian word for worst of the worst. She'd been watching my experiment over the top of the baby's bald head. It had stopped crying and was mouthing the medallion on Naunet's necklace.

"You're right. We'll put it on the fire with those creatures. Let it burn as well."

I dragged the bodies away. All the wood was still wet from last night's rain so I went into the cave to see if they'd kept any stored. The torches in the walls burned with a greenish glow, dipped in I dared not guess what kind of fat. I took one from the wall to guide my way past the stone walls gleaming with moisture. The sides of the passage were rubbed smooth as the inside of a lady's arm and I thought of those two hideous sisters pushing each other, jostling, complaining, bumping against the walls for the long years of their occupancy.

Beyond the passage, the cave widened out. Here were the filth-strew pits where they'd lived and slept. An unexpectedly pleasant smell of cooking, terrifying in the circumstances, drew me farther in toward their kitchen fire, where a natural chimney carried away the smoke. A pile of discarding clothing lay in the corner, all sizes from too-big for me down to a small girl's embroidered dress.

Their larder was just beyond.

I came out ahead of the fire I'd set, spilling oil and spreading dry straw in every corner of their lair. I only hoped it burned hot enough to cleanse my mind of what I'd seen. As I have said, it wasn't my first time to be the avenger of such horrible things. I hope it is my last.

Some dry straw and wood remained for us. Naunet glanced at me. She'd taken off her necklace and was dangling it for the baby. "You saw?"

"Yes and I'm sorry that you did."

"Such things should not be," she said, turning her head away.

"You're right there. It's over now, though."

She turned again to the baby with a bright smile, though her eyes sparkled more than before. "You're all right," she cooed to it, making up a little song. "You and me and Eno are all, all right."

Rolling a large stone in front of the cave mouth, I hoped both to seal in the heat and to hide forever the cave. There had been some gold and jewels flung down carelessly in there, for the fiendish sisters had not cared about such things. I didn't want treasure-hunters disturbing the site, not ever.

To lift her spirits, I kindled a fire for Naunet, then took away a burning branch to start another deeper in the woods, where the smoke and smell would not reach her. There was quite a bit of both at first. I had to hunt for the missing head. The eyes, though glazed, still held a look of living rage.

I started to throw the basket on the pyre as well, but something stayed my hand. I looked it over carefully, thinking that the decoration and the once-gay ribbons did not seem to be something a black-hearted creature would add to an incantation. It was a thing of craft, a useful item put to evil purposes. After a moment's hesitation, I put it down where the fire could not reach it.

I thought it would take forever for the bodies burn down. Within a few minutes, however, they'd begun to degrade, their trunks falling in with a loud hissing noise like the sea meeting a lava flow. I added the punky hearts of some rotten logs to increase the heat. The creatures seemed to dry and crack to flinders, breaking down quickly into flakes and ash. Even the heads were reduced to nothing.

Why did I stay and watch this vile cremation? Though I knew they were dead, even the one I hadn't decapitated, I had a sneaking, creeping feeling that they might suddenly leap off the fire and come back to the attack. They'd been hungry when they'd died. I thought of Naunet's idea of a starving ghost and that was enough to keep me watching with keen attention until the bodies were utterly consumed.

There were enough fallen leaves to spread around to cover up the blackened earth. I had little hope that anything would ever grow there again.

When I'd finished, I went to find their source of water.

I guessed that I was about two-thirds of the way up the Black Mountain. The water that poured from the rock above came down to fill a deep pool, hemmed in by rocks and moss, trickling away slowly down the far side again. It was so cold it was like running full tilt into a stone wall. Everything turned numb as I dove again and again to clean off both sight and smell.

Pulling myself out, I rubbed my face and hands vigorously and wrung the water from my kilt. I sat for a while, letting the sun be my masseuse. There were new troubles ahead but I was content to be without thought for a while. Only the cry of an eagle far above reminded me that I had responsibilities to others besides myself. And Naunet would probably like to have a wash as well.

At the corner of my eye, I saw a flicker of motion. I didn't whip around or shout but turned with natural ease to glance upwards as if in search of that eagle. I swept the view from earth to sky. I saw no one.

Yet I had a deep feeling that the woods were looking back at me. It was a feeling similar to one I'd met with before, for my protection when approaching a place of great evil. This was more like the land was studying me, determining my place and intentions.

Landscape has a life of its own, sometimes. Of course, it is populated by naiads in water and dryads in trees and sylphs of the air. You've got nymphs, fauns and centaurs, all dancing to the piping of Great Pan, the one god I never want to meet.

Beyond the spirits of the land, there is a deeper aliveness in the earth and the air. Something older even than the first gods, that remains half-aware and often amused by us little mortals. I notice this most of all in the sea. An awareness of the water itself, that has nothing to do with Poseidon and the rest of his crew. Why else does a wave always hit you just when your mouth is open?

I walked away from the Hag's Pool. At the site of the burning, I saw two hefty crows, gleaming of wing, wicked of eye. They seemed to be waiting for the heat to die down, pacing at the edges of the blackened ground.

"Get away," I said, waving my arm. They flapped their wings half-heartedly, watching to be sure I did nothing more threatening, like stoop for a stone.

"You don't want to eat anything from here," I said conversationally. "A nip of an eyeball from one of them would bleach your feathers."

A chatter from many voices arose from behind me. I glanced over my shoulder. The cluster of silver poplar trees seemed spangled as the lighter undersides of their leaves flirted with a breeze. Where they were not pale green, they were black as hundreds of crows perched among their branches. Never mind the Dead -- they were enough to strip the bones of a living creature.

I tensed. But they weren't threatening. Preening, cawing, shuffling along the branches like old men in black cloaks, they seemed content to stay where they were. I was aware, however, of bright, yellow-rimmed eyes watching my every move as I left the clearing, basket in hand.

* * *

Naunet sat on the end of a log, dipping a corner of a clean rag into a pot and giving it to the baby to suck. When I stepped on a cracking stick, she stood up, baby under one arm, knife at the ready in the other hand. "I guess I am too many nerves," she said, sitting down again.

"I am too." I nodded at the pot. "What's that?"

She said a word I didn't know. Seeing my confusion, she translated haltingly. "Inside a melon...little things...rocks? Little growing things?"

"Seeds?"

She smiled at the baby. "Silly me to forget simple words. We take the melon seeds, boil them and squish them up to feed baby when a mother cannot."

"Smart," I said. "I'm glad you're here. I haven't got much experience with babies."

"You are a man." The amount of tolerant pity she could infuse into such a simple sentence came as a surprise. As I said, Greek ladies don't think of men that way. Or maybe they do and are just better at hiding it. I'm not more fond of myself than most men, though I have a decent respect for my abilities, yet all at once I felt that I was essentially useless.

Killing monsters? I'm your man. Nursing infants? That's all right, sister, you do it. And when it came to diapers, I'd bend down and kiss the sandals of any woman willing to take that task on. I can only assume that giving birth alters a woman's nose.

I squatted down to be on their level. The baby turned his head from the cloth to appraise me. He had brown eyes, a bump of a nose and large ears. I smiled. He turned instantly back to sucking on the cloth. I was of no interest.

"I don't want to stay here for the night," Naunet said. "Too many unquiet dead."

"You and I are in complete agreement about that. We're not far from the crest of the mountain. If we don't dawdle, we should be over the top and halfway down by morning."

"You want to continue...up?"

"I think so."

"Why? Surely it would be better to return the way we came and go around."

"I still want to go to my village as quickly as I can. A few days journeying...."

"And what of this one?" she said, stroking the baby's cheek. "His poor mother will be seeking him. To lose one's family is a tragedy."

"Once I'm done, we'll take him back to town. Someone there will know if anyone is looking for a child and if not, we'll find many men who'd adopt a son." I knew a lot of stories about orphans who grow up to be the long-lost son of a king. I could wish my own tale was common. A kidnapped son could be an honorable fellow, even if the Fates twisted his story to make him kill his father and marry his mother. The bastard son of a god, however, didn't have anything to be proud of.

I had been told by the eldest of the gods, just before I sent him back to the depths of the Underworld, that I had the blood of a god myself. This the Olympians had confirmed though none of them claimed me as a son. The sword I carried was the only evidence I possessed, given to me by a man who might have once glimpsed my father. Only my mother could tell me the whole truth, if she would.

Believe me, I don't want to be a demi-god. I've met a few and even the ones I liked weren't much. They tend to be spoiled, fond of themselves, and always running whining to daddy or mom when things go wrong. Their motto seems to be 'Do you know who my father is'? But here I was asking the same question. I had to know, one way or another. I just had to know.

"A pity there are no oracles in this land. We could ask them to ask the gods."

I took a moment to remember what we'd been talking about. "Oh, the baby. Yes, they could tell us all about him...if the gods were in a talkative mood."

"The gods of Egypt and the gods of the Great Green are the same in that," Naunet acknowledged wryly. "They say only what they will."

"Anyway, the danger's over. The Slipstone Pass won't be feared anymore."

She looked around with her clear amber eyes and shivered. "I wonder...."

Finishing the feeding, clearing up, cleaning the kid, took less time that I would have imagined. We were on our way, Naunet on the horse with the baby, me leading, in next to no time. The baby was not too fussy, falling asleep after playing with the fringed ends of Naunet's hair. She sang it an old Egyptian lullaby that was more than half a prayer of protection.

She would not permit me to hang the basket anywhere on the horse. So I carried it, empty, tied to my pack. It bumped my thigh continually, a reminder that I probably should have burned it just for convenience's sake.

There was only one road, steep and narrow. If we'd met anyone coming the other way, someone would have to back up or go over, for there was no space to pass. The wind had risen, driving the smell of rain over the mountain. I only hoped it would hold off until we'd begun our descent or that descent would be faster than either of us would want. The Pass is well-named.

Despite our lack of company, I did not feel as if we were alone. Every so often, above the wind rustling the trees, I would hear or think I heard the harsh caw of a crow.

About the third time I scanned the tree line, Naunet asked me about it. "Some new danger?" and her slim knife appeared in her hand.

"I don't know. But I will be glad to get out of the open."

She repeated the words, feeling them in her mouth as if they were some strange new fruit. "Out of the open...out of the open...but where is shelter to be found?"

"Not up here. I wish your horse was a donkey."

"That is not sensible. A horse is a fine thing, rare in my country."

"Donkeys are more sure-footed for this kind of territory. Your people use them more than horses, don't you?"

"Donkeys are not as nice to ride."

Naunet patted its neck as if to take away the sting of any insult. Her knife had slipped back into her belt. I wondered how and why a nicely brought up Theban girl had become so deft. She was unusual, that was certain.

"Be that as it may," I said, "we had better pick up the pace." But how could we out-pace something with wings?

There's a feeling I get when things are about to become spiritually weird. It's akin to the prickle under the skin I feel when battle is imminent. The excitement is under my scalp, though, with an attendant ripple down my back as though skull and spine were reaching some greater awakening.

I felt it now, even more strongly than I had back at the Hags. There'd been hardly time for the feeling to develop before I was hacking off heads. Now I felt that whatever was coming couldn't be answered with a sword.

The day was brightening and the views from the top of the pass were probably quite inspiring. All it engendered in me was a determination to get out of sight. I felt exposed and observed. We were above the tree-line, surrounded by nothing but big rocks and windswept earth.

As we crested the top and started downwards, I looked up at Naunet who was gently smiling at the baby. Whatever premonition of danger I had was not reaching her. "Listen," I said urgently. "If something happens...."

"What will happen?"

"I don't know. But if it does, it'll be obviously a wrong thing."

She shook her head, showing her incomprehension. I didn't get impatient as I hardly knew what I expected myself. "But if something does happen, don't worry about me. Just ride out as fast as you can. Do what it takes to get you and the baby off this mountain."

"But surely whatever is wrong has been left behind. Those awful women...you were so brave."

"It's my job." I rubbed the back of my neck, where the tingling was growing irksome. Expectation hastened into anticipation with every crow's croak. I wanted whatever was going to happen to be as soon as possible while I was still at a peak of readiness.

Then, stupidly, while scanning the sky for the return of the birds, I stepped on a rock that twisted beneath my foot. I tried to save my balance, arms whirling. Maybe that made it worse. I didn't just fall down. I flew forward as if pushed from behind and went down, ass over end, just where the path was steepest.

Like a boulder, I bounced from level to level, with nothing to catch to slow my descent. The pack on my back burst in one impact and I sowed my goods up and down the peak. I bashed an elbow against a stone and my head against another, jarring my teeth and setting my eyes to rattling like gamesters' dice in a cup. My thigh scraped over gravel. I swear my shoulders met my hip-bones for the first time ever. They did not like each other.

I slid to a stop on my back and lay there, gasping, my ears ringing like a copper bowl struck with a heavy mallet. My wits were scattered with my belongings all over the slope.

CHAPTER SIX

I lay on something hard, face-up, judging by the sunlight glowing red behind my eyelids. Small stings, like little stones, fell on me. Remembering my thought about being pecked to death by crows, I lifted a hand to shoo them away.

"Oh, praise Maat...you live!"

"Maat?" The name was vaguely familiar. Some girl, maybe? I tried to remember where we'd met.

The voice went on talking but I couldn't follow what it said. It seemed far away and was continually interrupted by the sighing noises in my head. It was as if I held the world's largest seashell to my ear. Pain too came and went like ever-cresting waves.

The small stings came back. I opened my eyes and gazed around, feeling no desire to move any other part of my body. As near as I could tell, I lay on a little shelf of rock at the foot of an overhanging cliff or wall. A few scraggly plants struggled for existence, growing straight out from the dirt. Some had been snapped, showing green breaks, by the passage of some heavy object from above. Me...I very slowly realized.

A stone at the top surrounded by hanging strands of vine called my name. I blinked, slow as a lizard, at the miracle.

Then the miracle dropped a few pebbles on me, stinging my chest and arm. "Wake up," it commanded.

I glanced down and saw quite a few small white stones littering my form. Apparently, the rock had been trying to wake me up for a while now. "What do you want?" I asked, my voice thick and strange.

"I can't bring you up again unless you help. You must tie this rope around you." It came down like one of her vines. The loop thumped me but I could hardly feel it.

Moving was not high on my list of things-to-be-done. I'd seen worse places to spend a couple of centuries. Not the most comfortable bed, perhaps, but I'd grow used to it after forty years or so. I sighed deeply and closed my eyes again.

"Eno? Eno!"

That name was familiar too. Big guy, prides himself on being more than just muscle, believes he has more sense and a clearer vision than most men...well, he wasn't going to drag me into any harebrained schemes. Nobody was paying *me* to fight their battles.

If it hadn't been for Naunet, I'd probably be there still, a bunch of bones whitened by eternity. Though I hadn't wanted her along, though I'd warned her against coming, I had a responsibility to her that I couldn't excuse with bruises and contusions. Besides, the longer I lay there, the harder it was going to be to move at all.

I leveraged myself up on my bashed elbows. The ledge was only just wide enough for me and beyond it was nothing but a long drop to the flat land below. I would have made a splash like a stone slung into mud. I'd been lucky.

My head cleared a bit. I'd bitten the inside of my cheek at some point. I spat out the blood, relieved to see that no teeth went with it. Nothing seemed broken except my dignity.

"Get up, my little Thracian warrior...." Though it was a light voice, merry as sunlight on the sea, the command in it brought me to my feet as though yanked upright by a chain through my backbone.

I knew that voice well, though we'd only met a few brief times. The Goddess of Love, Aphrodite herself, who'd taken an interest in my affairs. A *motherly* interest as her husband, lame Hephaestus, had made certain to tell me. That was the safest kind of interest, though even her gentlest affections could not always be considered a benefit.

"Are you better, Eno?" Naunet called down.

"Is anyone up there with you?"

"No. No one." I could now recognize 'the rock with vines' as her head peering over the cliff edge, her hair falling around her face. "Can you climb up?"

"Tie the rope to something strong. The saddle, maybe?"

"Yes, I did. You hold on. I'll walk the horse forward and we'll pull you up."

I raised a hand in acknowledgment. The back of it was scratched and all four fingers throbbed. I recalled bending them back toward my wrist as I tried to slow my descent. Now I opened and closed both fists, trying to find a little strength.

Hand over hand, I began to climb up, my legs straight out in front of me. Blood trickled from the deep parallel cuts on my thigh. I looked like I'd gone five rounds with a mad tiger from the Indus.

When I reached the top, Naunet grabbed at me as if I'd fall over again if she didn't. Truthfully, I was glad of the help. I lay like a dead cow on the short grass there at the cliff edge. Black spots sailed across the red lining of my lids.

"Drink a little of this," Naunet said, lifting my head with one gentle hand.

She'd found my wineskin, not burst, thanks be to Dionysus. Though the resinous swill burned my bitten cheek, it sent a surge of warmth through my skin, as though I stood before a glowing brazier. After another swallow, I wiped my mouth and studied the situation. At the foot of the pass, the road took a sharp turn toward the west. I had rolled across it and off the edge.

Looking up, I saw just how far I'd fallen, tracing my path by the scattered pieces from my pack. A dark splotch on a white boulder was from either my head, which still felt spongy, or from the bottle of unguent I'd intended for my mother's gift. A rippling movement like a white wing on a thorn bush was my best tunic, the chiton I'd had made just before leaving Piraeus. Soon the crows would scavenge the pig knuckles, flatbread and dried figs that had been intended for my dinner.

That reminded me. I looked skyward. The black spots had not been on my interior vision alone. Half a dozen of them wheeled in the empty air above where I'd fallen. Every so often, one would croak and, as if in reaction to that call, the pattern they took would change. Even as I watched, more came, swirling around in an errant breeze, as if dark leaves had come to life.

"We'd better be moving," I said, rising.

"I thought we would stay here. Shelter at the side of the road. You are not fit to travel."

"I'm all right."

"Men always say that. They are liars. We will pitch our tent here, by the side of the road. I will collect your things and light a fire."

"I'm not spending another night on this mountain."

"But your belongings...."

"If it were my head and...elbows...up there, I'd still want to leave."

"Elbows? Oh, you mean balls." She brought the word out with naive pride at her language skills.

"Yes, I do," I said. "Where's the baby?"

She turned the horse around. There the tike hung, slung in a makeshift carrier of twisted and knotted cloth, swaying on the far side of the saddle. He gave a toothless smile when he saw me but saved his widest grin for Naunet.

"Good, he's all ready to go. Mount up, Naunet."

"I don't think it is wise."

There were maybe fifty or more birds now, wheeling now in near silence, and every one of them watching us with sharp eyes. Either Naunet didn't see them or she thought this was how such birds behaved in 'The Great Green'.

I took her hand and led her to the saddle. "Mount up. We're leaving now."

She sighed heavily at my dictatorial ways. "At least we should bind up your leg."

"It's fine," I said, ignoring the stinging sharpness that sliced into me when so much as the passing breeze touched it. "I'll walk it off."

My kilt had come off the worst. Sliced and shredded, it only just continued to cover my modesty. No matter how I hitched it up, the hem brushed against the gash in my leg. The porous cloth dyed itself crimson with every step. Frankly, I was a little apprehensive about taking too close a look. Dirt and grit had undoubtedly imbedded itself in my flesh and I'd have the task of picking it out bit by bit. I'd had enough experience on the battlefield to know that small wounds could wind up killing your just as effectively as one big one. Gangrene isn't a smell you want to encourage.

Right now, though the birds worried me more than all the rest combined.

You'd be right to wonder why I was in such a sweat over some damfool birds.

(Alpha) There were some hundreds now, with more joining the flock every moment. (Beta) They behaved as no birds I'd ever seen, even the ones who'd gotten drunk off fermented berries. They circled in a great wheel, keeping pace with us. Some were even flying backwards. (Gamma) I'd accepted responsibility for Naunet and, by extension, the baby, when I'd lopped off the first Hag's head. I even felt some duty toward the horse. (Delta) I'd heard the voice of Aphrodite. It hadn't been a weird echo or the crump I'd taken to the head. It had been her. Though I willingly admit my admiration and worship, the truth is that trouble follows the gods. The more interest they take in you, the more trouble finds you. I wanted to be far away when the lightning struck.

We hastened on, the sun in our eyes. The horse's breath labored but I didn't dare stop to succor it. After a brief flat run, the road angled downward again. This time I kept a careful watch on every foot fall.

"Eno?" Naunet said, her voice throwing high like a small girl's.

I looked behind me. Above her, the crows flew slowly in a dense swirling circle, a shield of shadow. I heard no caw or croak, only the rustle of hundreds of wings.

Naunet bent low over the saddle, hauling the baby up to rest securely in her arms. "What does it mean?"

The black swirl, like a whirlpool in the sky, seemed to pulse closer. "Ride out," I said sharply.

She nodded and clapped her heels against the horse's sides. As she passed me, she reached out her free hand. I ignored it, hoping she'd think only that I focused so hard on the birds that I hadn't seen it. I tend to avoid tender gestures on the edge of battle; they are bad luck.

I drew my sword, the only belonging that had survived my unique mountain-descending technique entirely intact and in the proper place. This sword might have be the key to my identity but right then I would have traded it for a child's green-wood bow and a stone-tipped arrow. A cyclops' eye in the back of my head would have been helpful as well. I'd like to know how far away Naunet had gotten. The horse hadn't wanted to go above a trot.

Watching the birds go 'round, waiting for them to attack, I found myself swaying to the rhythm that made them move. I shook my head to clear it. Maybe the knock I'd taken was catching up to me for my eyes began to close, my head to nod, the point of my sword to fall. I caught myself back, just as my hand started to open.

With a shout of rage, I hurled my sword into the writhing heart of the massed birds. It passed through, straight and smooth and useless. I'd disarmed myself to no purpose.

I vowed aloud, "I'll wring your necks one at a time if need be."

I spoke too soon. The circle grew ragged, breaking apart into sections. Some birds flew away, others just vanished as quick as the light when you blow out a candle. After a moment, all were gone, leaving no trace but a feather floating down, cut in half.

Jogging back, I snatched up my sword from the ground, marveling once again at its unmatched sheen and balance. Striking the rocks had made no mark upon that glistening blade. Only the slight nick toward the hilt, gotten long ago according to the tale I had with it, marred the smooth gleaming steel. A feather-pattern had been beaten into the metal itself in forging.

"Eno!"

Without thought for my battered leg, I turned and sprinted toward the sound of her voice. Had the birds returned? Vanished in one place did not mean vanished in all.

Naunet had stopped or the horse had when the black figure in the long cloak appeared before her. The slight breeze always present in these hills had no power to sway even the leaf-edged ends of the cloth that covered it. The hood concealed the whole of the head and face.

If I had a shield, I could have ridden it down the hillside. Instead I half-ran, half-slid down to Naunet, not so out of control I couldn't stop in front of the horse, sword once more in my hand. "Who are you? What do you want?"

The face slowly lifted, to peer out from the depths of the hood. I had expected some nightmare of maggot-ridden eyes and peeling flesh. Instead, I saw a woman with a pleasant round face and long lush curls of an oiled black. One of the long twists had been sheared off at the level of her jaw. She reached up and tugged on the sundered tress.

"A brave man may be forgiven much," she muttered in heavily-accented Greek. "If your aim had been more true, I should be lying there with a slit throat."

"Who are you?" I demanded again. "Are you a spirit of these mountains? If so, let us go in peace. I have slain the Hags. If that displeases you, let us fight."

Her fathomless dark eyes widened. "Killed them? All of them?"

"He did not," Naunet said earnestly. "I hit the last one with a stone. You will not punish Eno alone."

"Punish him? My dear child, I am more likely to reward him." She flung the edges of her cloak over her shoulders. She wore a simple dress, belted at the waist with a cord, of a rusty black. Her hair coiled in long black ringlets dappled with peat-colored glints like river water, her arms bare and shapely, but her aura was that of an older woman.

"We have no affection for the Siren's Daughters. They had stopped people coming to consult us. Though we can grow much in our garden, we missed the extras people brought us for our services."

"Services?" Naunet leaned forward, her eyes intent. "Are you...an oracle?"

"We are oracles indeed, priestesses of the Great Apollo."

"Oh, what happiness! You must tell Eno his future. He won't believe me. He's going to save me...."

"What's with the birds?" I asked, interrupting, not so eager as Naunet to meddle with the woman.

"A gift of the god's. You would not have me bruise my feet on these hard stones?" Something about the glint in her eyes showed me my tumble had not been unwitnessed.

"And just who is 'we'?"

"My sister and I. We are fortunate to receive our great lord when he condescends to us. He tells us things; sometimes even that which we wish to know."

Naunet glanced at me expectantly. I already knew I had as much chance stopping the sun as keeping her from an oracle. Anyone who claimed to have an understanding of the future would find her eager and gullible.

"Very well," I said. "Lead on."

After the trick with the birds, I wasn't going to drop my guard for an instant. She might have other talents to show.

We followed her as the road began to switch back down the mountain. The horse seemed relieved. Naunet began to sing a lullaby to the baby. I wished she would stop as it set my teeth on edge. I felt the weight of the hag on my back, felt her stinking breath on the back of my neck.

Maybe I was distracted by those feelings but I missed the moment we passed from the rocky hillside to a hidden-away glade, peaceful and green. A wattle-and-daub cottage with a red thatched roof stood in the center, shaded and sheltered by a large leafy tree. Bean-stalks grew around a stone well, the scarlet and yellow flowers glowing like oil lamps among the leaves. Bees were busy in those flowers and among the blossoming herbs. Their humming resonated around the concealing cliffs. It was as calm a place as I had ever been which made me all the more wary. I am always waiting for the harshness within the honey and the steel beneath the silk.

"Lea!" Our guide called out as soon as we turned between two out-croppings of stone. "Lea? Guests!"

"It's better to be a guest than a present," Naunet murmured to me. I grunted in agreement, keeping my hand on my sword. If a slavering monstrosity came bounding out, I wanted to be ready.

"I'm here, Metta...I'm here." She thrust the covering over the door aside with her shoulder and had to duck her head to come out. Tall, her slender figure swathed in a rough brown robe, she carried a wooden tray, a thin slice of tree trunk by the look of it. Four wooden goblets and an earthenware ewer balanced precariously on it. "Honey-mead, anyone?"

"Oh, lovely! I could just do with a slug of that!" Metta hurried forward and took up a cup.

I watched them surreptitiously as I lifted Naunet down from the horse's back. "Don't drink," I whispered into her hair.

The horse promptly began to lip at a lush plot of grass, pushing aside a couple of small sheep. If danger waited for us here, his animal senses weren't picking it up. Or maybe he was just hungry.

"Don't be rude," Lea said. "Guests first."

She offered us the tray. Metta poured out the golden-brown wine, a froth of fermentation pouring from the lip, sparkling like a stream.

"To the future!" Lea tossed off the drink and smiled into my eyes as if she'd guess my suspicions. It was a dare but one I wasn't going to accept.

"Yes...may it be wonderful," Naunet said, taking a sip. "It is as good as the beer of Osiris!"

"High praise from a daughter of the Nile," Metta said. "Your people invented beer."

I let the liquid just touch my tongue. Despite my thirst and the rich, tempting flavor, I still didn't trust these two enough to swig any beverage they handed me. Had Naunet drunk deep, despite my warning?

"Are you really priestesses of Apollo?" Naunet asked eagerly.

They smiled at each other. Naunet and I looked more like members of the same family than these two. Metta's dark ringlets contrasted sharply with the smooth, slightly graying brown of her sister's hair. One was round and comfortable; the other tall and straight as a staff. They had similar smiles, though, knowing and wise, like amused mothers watching at the antics of their young.

"More mead?"

"And you must be hungry," Lea said, glancing at me in a measuring kind of way as if she were weighing me in some cosmic scale. Whether they were true pythonesses or not, they were disturbing on a spiritual level.

"I'll say he's hungry," Metta told her sister. "Do you know...you won't believe what this man has done. He has slain the Siren's Daughters!"

"What? All?"

"All."

Lea cast her eyes heavenward. "At last. Oh, you shall have such a feast! Tell me, quickly. Did you bury them?"

"They are burned," I said, not hiding my disapproval at this unseemly interest. "And their victims as well. We rescued this infant from their hands."

"Was there a basket?" Metta asked, eagerly. "With handles and colored strands woven around the edge? It looked ordinary. You might have overlooked it."

Naunet and I glanced at each other. What did this mean?

"I had it," I said.

The dark-haired woman looked eager as her sister brightened. "You did? Where is it now?"

"When I fell...it was tied to my pack. I don't know if it got crushed. But whether or not, it's still up there by the side of the road."

"Why does it matter?" Naunet asked. "It was a common enough thing."

Metta's shoulders moved beneath her robe, like a bird shaking out its feathers. "It is useful. They stole it from us, long, long ago. We wanted it back, that's all."

"Where did it come from? The gods?"

"Oh, no. Our other sister made it. But now she is dead and can never make another like it. We haven't the skill."

Why do Weird Sisters always come in sets of three?

"Who were they? The Siren's Daughters." I asked.

"Just what they sound like. They were the daughters of a Siren and the Great God Pan," Lea said. She no longer smiled slyly as if she were privy to a secret shared by her sister alone. She had paled and the tray she still held shook between her hands.

"He wanted to learn their songs," Metta added. "To understand their powers. One promised to tell him everything if he would give her children. The Hags were the result."

"Brave Pan," I mumbled.

"Foolish mortal. He did not love them but he will avenge them."

"But they were cannibals. The gods don't like cannibals."

"The gods do not. But Pan...how many of the animals under his care devour each other? No matter what these daughters did, they were his and he looks after his own."

Suddenly, the peace of the glade seemed ominous and watchful. Pan is the god of the Wild and, though this place was well-cultivated, even it had been untamed once upon a time. His memory might yet lurk under the leaves or among the woods.

"Sister," Metta said, "we had better prepare. Our god will be done with his work soon. We shall ask our questions at sunset."

Lea became our hostess, showing Naunet a place to bathe herself and the baby, who needed it badly. I sat, nursing my bruises, binding my gashed leg, in a patch of sunlight slanting among the stones. From time to time, I flicked a stone off my thumbnail, trying idly to hit a larger rock some slight distance away. This trip to visit my mother, undertaken in a determined spirit, had become all-too complicated.

But what could I have done? Hauled Naunet back to town bodily? She would have followed me again the moment I left her brother's residence. That mother of hers would have let her out. I wanted a word with that woman. Why didn't she keep her daughter decently at home where she couldn't drag innocent men into trouble...

I was trying and failing to work up a good grudge. Truth was, the path I'd chosen would have run me head on into the Hags even without Naunet, leaving me in the same position as I was now. But I could wish she hadn't hit that one on the head just when she'd been about to tell me...what? Lies? Truth? How would I ever know?

When sunset turned the glade golden, the women reappeared, Metta carrying the basket in one hand. I didn't ask how she'd gotten out there and back again so quickly, though I did reach out and brush a loose feather off the back of her robe.

"Thank you," she said, lifting the basket.

"It didn't get crushed?"

"The handle is broken but that it easily mended. It is a great relief to us to have it back."

"Why?" I asked, trying not to sound too suspicious.

"We keep bees, as you can hear. When we take the honey, we used to pop the bees into this basket to keep them peaceable. Without it, we were couldn't collect the honey without stings. Bad for us, bad for the bees."

"You can't just...." I twiddled my fingers in the air, miming magical powers.

Metta laughed. "No, I wish we could! My late sister had a calming influence on most things but even she could not make bees behave. She was the beloved of our god. Lea and I were only her handmaidens. But He is still kind to us in her memory."

"Apollo is said to have a short memory where women are concerned."

"Oh, that's true. But a short memory to a god is a life-time to you and I."

They dragged out a column, as high as my knee, in the last of the sunlight. On top, they placed a shallow basin, half-filled with water from the well. As darkness gathered, seeming to seep out of the sheltering cliffs, they lit small candles and set them to float upon the water. Their light shimmered on our faces as the candles drifted. Naunet's eyes were huge and she smiled with child-like excitement, watching the priestesses.

They'd put their hands on their eyes, swaying back and forth as they began to chant, each in a different tempo. The two chants twined together, twisting like threads to create something new.

The language had words that sounded vaguely familiar but most of it was incomprehensible. Eventually, I realized that I was hearing Minoan, a language that had died years ago when the island of Minos blew up in a volcanic explosion of wrath. Where had Metta and Lea and their un-named sister come from and just how old were they?

After a bit, one voice died away, leaving the other to carry on. I was reminded of the way a top will go on spinning for a long time after the cord has been pulled away. Eventually, it too faded away.

I opened eyes I didn't remember closing, to find Lea standing before me with her tray again in her hands. "Pour a goblet full," she said, "and spill it for our god. Then pour another and drink." One eye closed in a wry wink. "A real drink this time, eh?"

The libation made, I did as I was told. Whether the wine was drugged or poisoned or pure, I was committed to this. "To the Sun-god," I said and drained the cup to the last drop.

Again the chanting, faster and more intense. Maybe it was the drink or a trick of the shimmering light that fooled my eyes into seeing a glowing orb begin to gather and strengthen above the basin. The water had gone from black to the silver of moonlight, sparkles playing on the surface. Then around each candle, molten gold began to grow, too bright to look upon. It spread outward from candle to candle, touching, melding, brightening.

A discord struck across the chants of the women, like the chiming of a tarnished bell. Metta gestured to Naunet and I to kneel down. We did, while the two priestesses held their hands out over the now-burning water. In Greek, they chanted, "Hear our prayer, Radiant One! Hear us. Answer us. Protect this man and this woman. Return the child. Hear us. Answer us."

CHAPTER SEVEN

"You've done it this time, Eno, my friend."

He lounged on a throne draped with golden lion skins. Eight or ten beautiful maidens and equally beautiful young men stood beside him, waiting to offer a towel, wine, fruit, sparkling water or whatever the god desired.

"What have I done, Lord?" I asked.

"We're pleased, of course, that you destroyed those dreadful creatures. They had some nasty habits. But Pan, alas, is angry with you."

"That's what I hear."

Apollo is the god of all that is civilized. Music, art, light and beauty are his responsibility and delight. He drives the chariot of the Sun across the skyfield, though lately he's been farming the job out to Helios. Apollo is a hospitable god, fond of good living and bodily comforts. He is also jealous, exacting and vain.

He rose and came down the steps of his throne, inlaid with blue lapis and glittering sunstone. He took a goblet from an offered tray and held it out to me. "Take a good drink. It will be several days before you have another."

I pledged him as I lifted it. The true Hippocrene, the wine of poets and singers, slipped down my throat as smoothly as water but with a kick like molten lava. "I'm in real trouble, then?"

"Oh, yeah."

He wore a white linen mantle edged with sheaves of wheat worked in glittering thread. An amber goatee of several weeks' growth sprouted on his chin, obviously there to disguise a slight softening of the jaw-line.

"What can I do?"

"Nothing. For now. Pan is too angry for apologies or reason. Not that he's ever amenable to such things at the best of times. Might as well try to talk sense into a tidal wave."

Apollo reached out for the tray on his other side, piled high with lush purple grapes. A moment's frown on the god's forehead and the grapes changed to perfectly ripened pears. He tossed me one and bit into another. He had really good teeth.

I thought it best to do the same. The flavor was the distilled perfection of the best pears ever grown, sweet and grass-scented. Another five minutes and it would have been overly ripe; five minutes earlier it would have been too hard. I knew I'd never fancy another one and pears used to be my favorite fruit.

"If Pan pursues me," I said, prompting him.

"My beloved sister will try to talk to Pan. They get along, you know. All that running around in the woods like savages." He shuddered. "No hot food. No proper bathing facilities. And bugs in everything. They say it's 'fun'."

"Sometimes it is a necessity."

"Oh, I understand that. Pressures of campaign and whatnot. But to deliberately subject oneself to filth and rough-living? Why work one's immortality away trying to improve conditions only to have some people decide on barbarity?"

The nearest server, a maiden of glowing skin and rippling golden hair, poured me a refresher of the deep red wine. The fragrance that arose spoke of warm summer days, eating wild berries under a cloudless sky. Scents of lily and rose drifting windingly from the goblet. It was not the same as before. Hippocrene wine I'd had occasionally back home, though it cost what I got for dispatching a smaller dragons. Mindful of the pear, I did not drink. The world has few enough consolations without me losing my taste for wine.

Apollo patted me on the shoulder and returned to his throne. "You'd better make for a civilized city just as soon as you can. Pan can do too much to you if you keep wandering around in the Wild."

"We're going to Kalithanos."

"Kalithanos hardly qualifies as the sort of metropolis I had in mind. They don't even have a decent theater!" He stroked his goatee. "I suggest you got back to Athens. Avoid all green spaces. Stick to civilized pavements and don't go out by night."

"I've been offered a job in Egypt," I said.

"Egypt? Oh, I love Egypt. There's this funny little shop in Memphis where you can get really good deals on incense, the good stuff, if you know what I mean. Of course, you should have been there a thousand years ago before all the tourists came. That's when you saw the real Egypt."

"But it is civilized."

"Oh, certainly. Pan can't stand the place. They have chairs."

The servitor took the heavily chased goblet from me as Apollo and his court began to recede from my sight. The scene shrank, becoming enclosed in a ball of pure crystal which turned to sparkling flares and whirled away into the sky.

I lay on my back with the sun on my face, aware of the heat and light through my closed eyelids.

"Well, *that* was weird," Naunet said. She sat back on her heels, her arms crossed. Her pretty face was dirty again.

"Oh?" I sat up, putting up a hand to explore a painful spot on the back of my head.

"You stood up in the middle of the reading, said "What have I done, my lord?" and then fell over, whack! All of a piece, like a felled palm tree."

"What did our hostesses do? And where have they gone?"

"They are very irritating women. One lifted your eyelid, said that you were with the god and went off to tend their goats or their bees or some such thing. It is not how we behave in Egypt."

I was still dreamy. "What did you do?"

"I wailed and poured dirt on my head, beseeching the god to release you. And it worked." She looked both surprised and worried by her new-found powers.

"He would have let me go anyway. I'm nowhere near pretty enough to serve in that court."

"I think you are very pretty," Naunet said loyally.

"Thank you." But I was a spotty, saggy pile of decrepitude compared to the effortless young athletes of Apollo's retinue.

I'd slept through an entire day, it seemed. The sun I saw was glowing red as it sank behind the hills. A rising moon was dyed a pinkish gold as it swam upward into the evening sky. A breeze set the leaves to rustling as Naunet brought me a new-baked loaf of bread and some honey. The flavor awakened my taste for mortal food.

Our hostesses returned, carrying low burning torches. "The bees say trouble is coming," Metta said gravely.

"The bees?" Naunet asked.

"They travel far and talk to many creatures and plants. They learn much just from listening to the wind."

I stopped Naunet's scoffing mid-snort. "That makes sense. The flocks knew when there was a wolf or a bear around long before we shepherds did. Bees are just another kinds of flock, right?"

Lea nodded. "You may stay tonight. But tomorrow you must hasten from the mountain."

"The god said..." I began, but felt that the two wise women already knew what I was going to say.

Naunet didn't. "Yes? What did he say?"

"That my safety lay in returning to more civilized corners of the world."

"Like Egypt?" Her eyes began to glow.

"Yes. Like Egypt."

"Come," Lea urged. "Let me show you where you may rest." Glancing skyward, she reached out for her sister's hand. "Inside, I think, and quickly."

I saw nothing but wasn't going to doubt their superior senses. This was their territory, not mine.

Three winks, a couple of nods and one emphatic gesture later, I made them understand that Naunet and I should sleep separately. I heard Lea and Metta giggling like little girls about it later. It was harder to separate Naunet from the baby but they took him from her mid-yawn and she was too worn out to argue.

* * *

Of course, I couldn't sleep. I'd been out cold for most of the day already. I felt as restless as a bull-leaper five minutes before show time. The air in the small lean-to off the side of the hut seemed stale, despite the gaps that let the moonlight shine through. The straw of my bed poked me in the back of the neck. The dust stuffed my nose. I scratched, I wriggled, I swore.

Finally, with a muted roar, I rose up, took my sword, and walked out into the night. Outside, night-blooming flowers offered their scent, perfuming the night with sweetness. The moon, glimpsed through veiling clouds, had a soft shimmer that seemed to settle like gleaming oil over every surface and shape. A far-off breeze disturbed the tops of the trees, sending a faint shiver through the air. All seemed peaceful.

Wandering on, I found myself among the shapely boles of elderwood trees. Something regular in their spacing told me that this was no wild, chance-grown wood but a grove almost like a farm. The trees were tall and impeccably pruned. How long had Metta and her sister tended this patch of land, to tame even the trees?

The night grew darker as I walked under the branches, the light from the sky reaching through in broken beams. I heard the wind again, sighing and whispering on high. All around me, the night began to gather, invisible yet palpable like a mist or smoke. It seemed to blow around me, moving my clothes, brushing over my close-cropped head like a hand.

Fallen leaves swirled and tossed, spinning in the scattered moonlight. The scent of the air became heavier, more like musk now than flowers. I thought it high time I turned back.

I thought I heard laughter, like that of Metta and Lea, but with a cruel under-note. The blowing leaves seemed to twirl up in small cyclones, taking on a human shape. I saw faces leering at me from the crux of limb and trunk. The moonlight wavered as though half-seen spirits walked among the grasping branches. Drawing my sword, I turned about cautiously. Whatever I saw moving out of the corner of my eye vanished as soon as I looked straight at it.

Useless though the question always proved, I couldn't keep the words "Is anyone there?" from my tongue. No answer came back, of course.

Another few steps. Then, just as I realized I didn't know which way I'd come, the terror hit me. I felt a burning madness in my head, as if an army of evil spirits riding nightmares were attacking me with a battering ram made up of all the fears I kept at bay. I broke out in a drenching of cold sweat as I struggled with an urge to run, run away from this horror that seemed to fill everything I saw, every breath I drew. I knew, though, that if I started running, I'd never stop 'til I dropped dead with a bursting heart.

Any hero who claims to be fearless is a fool. Fear and I are old companions. I think of it almost as another sense, as vital as ears or eyes or the half-felt knowledge that alerts me when I am being followed or watched. But this wasn't fear...this was Panic.

With the last vestige of my sanity, I dropped to my knees, gripping the hilt of my sword between my clasped hands with all my strength. The decorative pattern of stylized clouds on the cross-piece impressed themselves so deeply that I could still see them in the morning.

The pain drove out the panic. The leaves still blew against me, but they were now only leaves, no longer forming themselves into figures of every monster I'd ever fought. If there had been anything else there, it had gone.

"Nice try, Pan," I said defiantly. For Panic, fear of the woods and the dark, is his tool. Countless lives had been lost to the wild maddened run, taking the panicked one over a cliff, into a raging river, in front of a loaded wagon. It comes on you when you are alone, when the night closes in. Woods are not human places, even when they've been cultivated. Even gardens can be profoundly spooky.

I'd been a fool to forget it.

In the morning, we left almost before the dawn. The two sisters were quiet, wrapped in dark cloaks that were pinned with the symbol of their god. They offered us bowls of porridge, swirled with honey and milk. It seemed less a breakfast than a ceremony.

"Go in peace, go with care," Lea intoned.

"Above all, go swiftly," Metta added. "It would be best to spend no more than a single night on the road."

I thanked them for their hospitality and help. Naunet gave each an impulsive, loving embrace. Lea tucked a few flowers into the girl's braids, while Metta pinned a black feather to the shoulder of her coat. They offered me no such talismans.

We'd not gone far when I turned back to wave a last farewell. But the entrance to their little realm had vanished. I wondered if just anyone could find it if the two who dwelt there did not wish it.

My visit to Apollo had advanced the healing of my scrapes, cuts and bruises by about two weeks. The richest of my bruises had faded overnight from the purple of ripe grapes to the sickly yellow-green of grass under a rock. Wherever I'd scraped skin away, pale pink patches glowed against my tan hide so that I looked like an odd kind of giraffe.

Naunet noticed me gingerly examining my forearms. They were still tender. Maybe I should have drunk the wine to finish the process but I didn't complain. At least I wasn't sore or bleeding. Though some spots itched like blazes.

"Do you often visit your gods?" she asked.

"It's not an invitation you can refuse."

"This Apollo...who is he?"

"He looks after the Sun, mostly."

"Ah. Like Ra."

There's nothing like a few rounds of *Who's Got The Strangest God* to make a journey pass quickly. "Not exactly. He also is god of healers, athletes, musicians, poets and swans."

"Swans?"

"Some say he and his sister Artemis were born from an egg. It's a long story."

I realized Naunet put a little extra distance between us. "I thought you liked oracles," I said. "Apollo is the god of prophecy, too."

"Oracles, yes. But this is a miracle. Gods do not behave so in Egypt."

"I know. That's one reason why I'm suddenly looking forward to the trip."

She smiled at that. "After you have been in Egypt for a time, you will want to change your gods for ours. Thoth in not unlike this Apollo but he stays on his side of the River and we stay on ours."

"The Nile?"

"Yes, the Nile. But also the river that brings us to our judgment. It flows into the World Beyond, the Field of Reeds, the Golden Lands. The all-encircling river where Ra sails the boat of the Sun."

"Your gods live there, I guess. Like mine on Mount Olympus."

"They live in their temples and everywhere. But they stay on the other side of the River."

The religion of the Egyptians never made any sense to me. I have heard at least six different stories for their Creation, all from the mouth of a trader I used to know well. He believed them all with equal fervor, even when they flatly contradicted each other. To him, they were all true. The rest of their faith is the same way. The Sun traverses the sky in the person of Ra, as a ship, as a chariot, as a dung-beetle rolling the golden orb ever onward. Ra Himself had been born, I was told, from an egg, from a lotus-blossom, from his mother the Sky, and from the headwaters of the Nile. Perhaps they were all metaphors for some other story entirely.

But a people who can believe six different Creation stories all at the same time with perfect faith in each would always be beyond my understanding. It explains a lot, however.

Take twenty thousand men. Tell them you need a pyramid. Every single one of them would have a different reason for building it but each one could give his entire effort in the service of that idea. The eventual glory of the Pharaoh would just be a side benefit which wouldn't matter nearly so much as the fulfillment of each man's private purpose. There are many pyramids in the Red and Black Land.

"So what are you doing in Kalithanos anyway? It's not exactly high on anybody's 'must-see' list."

"Oh, no," Naunet said. "It's a dreadful city, hardly worth the name. But my uncle, the High Priest, sent my brother here to negotiate a trade deal with the Hittites. He thought Hebnetma needed some experience of other cultures, other places. The Hittites chose Kalithanos and so we came. They are mere barbarians but my uncle thought it best if we be polite."

"Usually the Hittites come to you?"

"Everyone comes to Egypt." Her head lifted proudly. "Mother didn't wish for Hebnetma to go alone, nor did she want me to stay behind. My ghost, you know."

"Ah, yes, your ghost. I'll try to sort him out for you while I'm there. Do you know why your uncle wants to hire me?"

"No. But he looked frightened when we said good-bye at the docks. He never looked that way before."

I didn't sleep that night. I thought it best to stay on alert, sitting beside a fire I kept very bright. Darkness and loneliness were key to the onset on panic. I wasn't about to suffer another bout. I might not win this time.

In the morning, I made the mistake of commenting that the baby didn't look well. He was fussy, turning his head away from the cloth soaked in goat's milk that the two women of the glade had jugged for him. "Is he all right? He looks a little thin."

"He's fine," Naunet said, juggling baby, rag, and jug. "Here...you hold him!"

He went from being fussy to screaming between one breath and the next. I tried holding him on my shoulder, under an arm, on his back, on his front, and sideways. Nothing soothed him. I'd never felt so big or so clumsy. "Is he growing a tooth?" I asked.

"No, he's too young. I think he's hungry, but he won't take anything!"

Her tears mingled with the baby's as we headed down toward the well. We started meeting up with people again, every one of which had advice to offer 'the young couple'. Even when the baby nodded off, exhausted, people still wanted to talk about everything we were doing wrong. By the time we'd passed the third caravan, the horse had begun to walk faster as if he too were tired of unsolicited advice.

Naunet's calm temper began to wear thin by the time we reached the gates of the city. The baby had awakened some time earlier and had changed his wailing for a constant mewling that was not an improvement. It shredded our nerves all the more as there seemed nothing to do for him.

As we approached Kalithanos, a red sun was setting over the sea beyond the city. Several caravans had met up and a crowd gathered while the three leaders disputed, with stamping and spitting, who had the right-of-way. Threading my way among the people and beasts of burden, I'd walked on several steps before realizing Naunet's horse was no longer beside me.

She'd drawn rein and was gazing down at the baby in her arms with a look of such profound sadness that I felt a thud in my chest as if my heart had jerked. "What's wrong?" I demanded. "Is he...?"

"Look there," she answered, pointing with her chin. "Beside the gate."

Several people stood there, two men and a woman. They wore the dark, rough clothes of hill-people, my people. One of the men and the woman seemed to be arguing, or at any rate, he was. To whatever he said, she shook her head, sadly but firmly. A moment after I noticed them, she held up her hand as if to say 'enough' and turned away.

She started talking to people among the caravans with a kind of weary determination, her hands pressed together as if in supplication. The man reached out toward her, not in anger but tenderly. The other man covered his eyes with his hands as though he were weeping.

"Beggars," I said. "Nothing strange in that."

"No." Naunet slid from the horse's back and started toward the woman. "Her dress is stained with milk."

I followed, perforce.

Naunet was right. As soon as the woman saw the baby, she dropped to her knees as if someone had cut her sinews. Her dialect was strange to me, though some of the words sounded as if I should know their meaning.

Naunet placed the boy in his mother's arms. The distressed sounds stopped instantly as he began to root in her dress for sustenance.

The man, the boy's father I guessed, came running. He also dropped to his knees, gazing with tear-filled eyes at his son. He looked up at Naunet, standing like an golden goddess in the slanting sunlight, and bowed his head down into the dust. I was hard-pressed not to do the same. She seemed to have grown in stature far beyond than the naive young thing who followed me from this city several days earlier.

His Greek was better than his wife's but still halting. They'd lost the child, or it had been stolen, during their trip down from the mountains.

"We found him there," I said in Maedi, speaking slowly. Whatever language was interspersed with his Greek was not one I recognized. But there are many dialects in the mountains, where one tribe might not see another for years. Maedi is about as close to a common tongue as you will find up there.

At the first syllables, though, he jumped to his feet, standing protectively over his wife and nursing child. He said quite clearly, "We're not going back."

The other man had reached us by now. He put his hand on the first man's arm as if to reassure him. There was a distinct family resemblance in their small noses and firm chins. They wore their dark hair unusually long, swept back from high foreheads. His Greek was good. "A thousand thanks, stranger, for returning this child to us. Wherever did you find him?"

"That's a long story. He is yours?"

"My nephew. His mother would not accept that the child was lost forever. She has been asking every caravan, every passer-by, if he was seen. Even my brother had given up hope. The faith of women surpasses us all, yes?"

"Where did you lose him?"

"Close to wherever you found him!" He laughed, a strange laugh more like a horse's whinny than anything human. His brother still stood defiantly, legs apart, fists clenched. I smiled at him.

More to the point, so did Naunet. He couldn't stay angry or fearful when a seeming goddess smiled at him. "I am very happy," she said, simplifying her speech so he could follow easily. "He is a good baby."

She took the reins from my hand and offered them to the father. "Here, this is for you."

"For...?"

"Yes, take care of him. He is an excellent horse. We are leaving the city and I don't think he'd like a sea-journey."

"But this is a fortune you offer us," the older brother said.

Naunet neither nodded nor shrugged but somehow did both. "Take care of him," she said again, looking toward the child. Then she walked away. I followed after a moment spent stripping her bags from the weary animal.

The mother gave her son quickly to her man and hastened after Naunet. She touched the girl on the arm, immediately apologizing with pulled-back, raised hands. "My name...Bera."

Looking at the hands before her face, she began to pull at one toil-roughed finger, drawing off a ring made of bronze, twisted in a long spiral into the shape of a serpent. She pressed it into Naunet's hand. "To...to help."

"Oh, I can't," Naunet began but I muttered, "Take it. Say thank you."

My Egyptian lady slipped the ring onto her slim forefinger. Gracefully, lithely, she bowed as to a great queen. "I shall wear it always."

And so far as I know, she always did.

CHAPTER EIGHT

True to his code, Hebnetma showed neither pleasure nor surprise at my return. He clapped his hands and sent a servant for the captain of his ship. "We sail tomorrow at whatever time is best," he said. "When would that be?"

The captain had a military air that suited his lined face and far-gazing eyes. "We sail at your pleasure, my lord."

"Then be ready at first light. We have spent enough time in this city."

The captain struck his firm chest a mighty thump. "I obey." Definitely military.

Hebnetma glanced at me as though to be sure I'd taken note of this proper form. "You should prepare yourself for the journey."

"Uh-huh." I smiled but realized it was foolish to tease the boy. A good part of his pomposity came from his youth, putting on an elderly dignity purely to prevent others from treating him like the boy he was. "I wondered about the matter of payment. It's a long way to Egypt. I want to be sure I'll be able to leave, even if I don't take the job."

"That will be provided for," he said grandly. "You will be in my service until we reach my uncle. Then you will pass into his. If you choose not to take on the 'job', I will take you on again and it will be my responsibility to see that you are returned hence."

"Then a retainer is usual in these matters."

"A what?" For an instant, he looked confused. But he clapped his dignity back into place like armor.

"A small fee to hold my services in readiness."

"But you have said...very well." I could almost hear him think 'barbarian' but perhaps negotiating with the Hittites had taught him not to show everything he thought. "My personal treasury is already aboard the ship," he deigned to explain. "Will the morning be time enough?"

I remembered the chest of treasure he'd shown me on our first acquaintance. "Excellently. Now, I should like to retire for a bath."

His noble nose twitched despite himself and I knew he agreed.

I ate that night with the two bodyguards. Taller was named Fjuti and Broader was Takelot. Though they weren't symposium-quality conversationalists under any circumstances, a sort of heavy, knowing silence filled our first meal together. Between that and the giggling of handmaidens as they served our dinner, I wondered what gossip was spreading about Naunet and me and our jaunt in the hills.

I couldn't refer to it, of course. So I asked other questions. "Have you been a long time in this family?"

Takelot swallowed an olive. "Only this trip. Usually we serve in the High Priest's household."

"A high honor."

"Not to us. Our families have always served the True Line."

Fjuti reached for the beaker of wine and poured one for me and then for himself. He drank without noticeable pleasure, as though it were vinegar. "Give me good Egyptian beer," he said and added, "We're thinking of making a change. Our mothers have taken a place in Thebes. They used do mending for the ladies of the Royal House down in Tanis but they moved. Not so much work there now. The Royal House doesn't need so many guards now, either."

Despite their close resemblance, they were not brothers but double cousins. Their fathers, who had been brothers, each married one of a pair of sisters. Takelot and Fjuti were only weeks apart in age. They laughingly referred to each other as 'runt' or 'bantam' and told me that their fathers had been men of the Royal Guard where their older brothers still served. That meant that their families were among the largest and strongest men who ever lived, for the Egyptian Pharaohs had gone into Nubia for their guards, choosing only the best that noble nation had to offer. The Medjai were a fighting force fit to take on any in the world, solely dedicated to their Lord and to each other.

Takelot sighed, whether from repletion after a good meal or from nostalgia. "We're too little for the standard service and now that our mothers have left Tanis, there's no reason for us to return."

"Besides, there's an opening in the Archers for a couple of good men," his cousin added. "Honorable, peaceable work."

"The archers?" Though they'd neither have trouble stringing a bow, I didn't see how they'd ever fire one without snapping it in two. I had trouble myself and I wasn't in their league.

"The police," Fjuti explained. "Nice quiet duties. Walking through the street, checking that doors are shut and that malefactors captured. Sounds good."

"'Course we'll have to work the graveyard shift for a bit, til we get promoted."

"It won't be long. We'll capture a couple of tomb raiders and Ptah's your uncle. Then we're out of the City of the Dead and picking up a few spare coins from grateful citizens."

Across the Nile from Thebes, and almost equal to it in size, stood a silent necropolis where less ambitious grave-robbers plied their trade. The police were kept busy watching for them. Even quite ordinary citizens were buried with enough valuables to make a quick dig worthwhile. The more noble the corpse, of course, the better the haul. But being too ambitious, with an eye to a royal tomb, lead to exposure, torture, and a slow death at the request of the judges. Still, it was said that few of the great pharaohs or their wives kept for long the grave goods that were sent with them to eternity. Judges, after all, are only human and no less amenable to a bribe than other men.

"Times are tough," Fjuti added. "Lots more robbing going on now, or so our cousin Ya tells us. He's been in the Archers for a couple of years, just got promoted to constable, but he says they're always looking for a few good men."

"You should come with us," Takelot offered. "We'll introduce you to Ya. Steady work. Regular pay. And nothing to worry about as long as you stay close to the oil lamp."

Fjuti grimaced as if his cousin had dropped a brick on his foot. I glanced at the oil lamp that sat upon our table, gilding the empty dishes and gnawed bones with a light too beautiful for such mundane things. "So you do know what's going on."

With elaborate ease, Takelot walked to the doorway of our little room. He yawned and stretched there and only, as if by chance, glanced up and down the hall. Meanwhile, Fjuti, with much less false show, opened the other door to the courtyard behind the house. The croaking of the frogs that lived there got a little louder.

They came back and seated themselves. Fjuti scraped a finger along the base of a bowl that had held hummus and moodily licked off the residue. "We don't know much, Eno. Just rumors and whispers in the wind. But as we are all Brothers of the Blades, eh?"

I nodded. Forever acknowledged was the bond between men who had taken arms in formal service, even if for different armies and for opposing kings. "Does this have anything to do with ghosts?"

"No. Why, what have you heard?"

"You first."

A moth had come in and flew lazily around the lamp. The shadow of its wings on the walls grew and shrank as it toyed with the notion that it could come near the flame and not get burned.

Fjuti sucked his teeth in lieu of any more hummus. "Do you take any interest in politics?"

"When there's a profit in it, I do."

"A couple of years ago -- stop me if you've heard all this?" I hummed encouragingly and he continued. "A couple of years ago, Pharaoh decreed that Lower Egypt would henceforth be rules by a general and Upper Egypt by the High Priest of Amun, our young puff-guts' uncle."

"Why did he do that?"

They shrugged gleaming shoulders simultaneously. "Who questions Ramesses the Great?" Takelot asked rhetorically.

"Wait a minute," I said. "I know a guy who said he was the personal tutor to Pharaoh's sons. He had fifty of 'em. Didn't they object to this general taking over?"

"Yeah, he did have fifty, once upon a time," Takelot said. His cousin closed a hand on the log-like arm on the table.

"Who's this 'tutor' character?"

"Phandros of Sparta."

"Oh, him." The two massive men smiled at each other in a reminiscent way. Fjuti laughed. "Your friend was never tutor to Pharaoh's sons, unless there were a few misbegotten by-blows among us."

"Among you?"

"He taught the sons of the Royal Guards to write our names, to read enough to understand our duties, to mind our manners. He didn't stay long but we liked him."

"Aye," Takelot said. "T'was drink that did him down. But he taught us some clever tricks of the warriors' trade, for all he seemed no stronger than a reed."

Even a weedy, reluctant Spartan would know enough to astonish an Achilles, let alone two future night watchmen.

"Go on with what you were saying about politics," I said. I felt that familiar sizzle in the pit of my stomach as I realized I was about to get the information I needed most.

"The fifty sons of Pharaoh are no more," he said in a whisper. "Some died of an odd fever. Still more were cut down by accidents, ate bad meat, or were thrown from a chariot. Others...others...." Takelot's deep voice slowed and I saw with surprise that sweat was beading on his forehead despite the cool evening air. "I saw one of them...before the Pharaoh set out his decree."

"What did you see?" I asked, pouring the last of the wine into his cup.

"A statue." The cup rattled against his teeth as he drank.

"A statue? But there are so many statues in Egypt. I've seen them myself. Ranks upon ranks of sphinxes or cats gods lining the roads to the temples."

"This one...this one stood alone. Looking over the river. The Prince would do that every night before bed. Go down to the banks and look toward the rising moon. He would pray to the Gods of the Nile and the Heavens to preserve his father's life another day."

His cousin continued. "Prince Thutemut never liked any of the guards hanging around him. They stayed within call but if he was going to cuddle some honey, he liked to woo alone. Maybe the guards should have ignored those orders. I don't know."

"If it was his fate to die, there would be nothing anyone could do about it," I said. "Second-guessing won't do any good."

They knew that as well as I did. They also knew it didn't help at all. You still blame yourself when a client dies. I still wasn't sure, however, what the statue that seemed to strike them with such horror had to do with dead princes. "So what happened to the Prince?"

"We were just kids," Takelot said, "We used to like to do a little night-fishing. Sneaking out, sneaking back in. Kid stuff. That night, we were coming back later than usual." His words dried on his lips.

Fjuti took up the tale. I couldn't be sure if this was all true, or a tale invented to give the new boy the shivers. "I heard a funny noise, like someone walking on gravel. But there was no gravel by this stretch of the river. Then a voice cried out. Young as we were, we ran to the rescue. Nobody was there. Except this statue, which had never been there before."

"There was enough moon to see his face," Takelot said. "It was definitely Prince Thutemut."

Did they have Gorgons in Egypt?

A sharp voice sounded from beyond the doorway. "What are you girls still doing up? You'll be fit for nothing in the morning and there will be much to do."

The two bodyguards were up and moving with a turn of speed unexpected in men of size with a good quantity of wine sloshing around their insides. Fjuti went out the back door and his cousin didn't stop even long enough to wipe the tears from his eyes. They didn't say a word of warning to me. So much for the Brotherhood of Blades.

Though I knew that nothing had happened between Naunet and me, I still felt like a burglar meeting a householder when her mother stepped into the room. She wore a wig of small braids, tiny jewels winking among the rich black locks. Her linen dress hung in folds from waist to hem, kept tight to her graceful figure with interwoven bands of blue and red cloth. Bangles marched up her left and right arms so that she was accompanied always by a tinkling as of bells.

The kohl she wore had settled into tiny lines around her eyes since it had been applied in the morning. She looked, consequently, more tired than her crisp words sounded. "I trust you have had all you want?"

"Yes, indeed." I stood up when she'd entered, but not to flee.

"And your chamber is to your satisfaction? I regret that so much of the furniture has been packed away. In ordinary circumstances, you would have had a bed, not merely a roll on the floor."

"I'm used to that," I said.

She inclined her head graciously, never showing that she expected nothing more of a barbarian like me. "Then will you follow me? The maids wish to clear away. They must finish packing as my son tells me we are leaving very early." Without waiting for my consent, she clapped her hands sharply.

Immediately the serving girls came in, bobbing at their mistress and smiling sidelong at me. The Lady walked out into the garden at the rear of the house. I followed her, taking the oil lamp from the table.

"Forgive me," I said. "I don't know your name."

"I am Meryt, She Whom Maat Is Pleased To Smile Upon. You may call me Meryt-Amun, as my brother-in-law has graciously taken us into his household upon the death of my husband."

"Was he one of the sons of Ramesses?" I asked.

She turned to me with a surprised and puzzled expression. "No, he was a corn-factor in the royal granary. That was before the Court returned to Tanis, of course."

"I see."

She put up a hand and eased the collar of beads she wore around the base of her throat. "Excuse me for speaking so sharply. My sister, you see, was wife in the second degree to Pharaoh's seventh son. My marriage was considered something of a mismatch. But we were very happy despite everything."

"I'm sure you were. And you have two handsome children to show for it."

She thanked me with an easy gesture of her long-fingered hand. Though claiming only to be a corn-factor's widow, she had all the mannerisms of a noble lady. I wondered if she'd been raised with the expectation of making a splendid marriage and if she hoped to live out that future through her daughter. But if that were so, why had she acquiesced to Naunet's going off with me, who could have been the barbarian ravisher who haunts all civilized nightmares?

I started to ask her about it, but she got in ahead of me. "My son tells me that you are a man of wide experience, so much so that my brother-in-law has asked for your services expressly."

"That's what he tells me, too, though I haven't any hint of what the High Priest wants me to do. Do you know?"

"I? No, he confides very little to me. I do not live in the Temple and do not see him often."

I remembered that in Egypt belong to a 'household' didn't necessarily mean residing in a house, only that the master of the house had promised to take responsibility for you. In return, you tried not to disgrace him and to give what service you could in return. I told myself to be sure to keep my status perfectly clear. No one but me needed to feel responsible for me.

I caught myself up at that point. If there was one thing I needed just then, it was several gods to be looking out for me. If I couldn't return to Greece or Thrace due to Pan's enmity, I might have to beg for a permanent job from the High Priest of Amun. I didn't look forward to it.

"There's always the graveyard shift," I muttered.

"Did you speak?"

"No, my lady. Being connected with the royal house, what can you tell me about some prince turning to stone?"

"Why, nothing. I've never heard of such a thing. It sounds like a tale for children."

"You're probably right. You hear a lot of strange rumors in my line of work."

"You must be good at what you do. My brother-in-law hires only the best. He should, he can afford to pay for it. No one questions his expenditures." A tinge of bitterness had colored her tone. I wondered if she attached herself and her daughter to this diplomatic mission in order to avoid paying her own bills for a few months.

"Pharaoh used to have a lot of sons, I hear."

Meryt busied herself in turning the bracelets on her arm so that the jewels all lined up. She flicked her eyes at me, as though weighing me. "Yes, it's tragic. I don't believe he's ever gotten over it. There are only a very few left, young ones, mostly. Pharaoh only shut himself off from his women-folk two years ago when he gave the palace to the General."

"All Egypt must pray for the safety of these young princes."

"Oh, we do," Meryt said fervently. "I have heard that almost the last two are returning home soon from a mission in Punt."

"Punt? That's one place I haven't been yet."

"It is fabulously rich, they say. Years ago, a queen came down the Nile from there. It was before I was born but my father told me of the ships heaped high with gifts for this pharaoh's divine father."

"That's right. Your kings are gods."

"That is true." She ran her hands over her upper arms as if suddenly cold. The wind had freshened a bit, for I could hear it searching mournfully along the walls of the town. But here, in this enclosed garden with the pool, it seemed warm enough. Yet she shivered.

"You should go in," I said in Egyptian. "I can find my way to my bed though I thank you for your graciousness."

"I would not have thought you would be so well-spoken," she answered in the same language.

"I am fond of learning new tongues." I bowed to her. As she passed me, I said suddenly, stopping her, "You are certain you've heard nothing about a prince turned to stone. It wasn't very long before you left on the journey to Kalithanos."

"No, I heard nothing of such a thing," Lady repeated with even more emphasis.

"So you said. Well, good-night, my lady."

She started to leave but I stopped her for the second time and said, "Just one more thing, if you don't mind."

On a deep sigh, Meryt turned around. Her formerly easy carriage hardened as she looked at me, her lips all but vanishing as she pressed them together. "Yes?"

"Why didn't you stop Naunet from following me up into the hills?"

"I did not know she had left the house until sometime after she had gone. If I had known of her plans, I would have indeed stopped her. Her behavior is shockingly unconventional. I can only be grateful that she met with a man who did not dishonor her." Her smile was brief.

"Naunet told me you both knew and encouraged her rash act."

"I can't imagine that she ever said such a thing. She may be a little headstrong at times, but she is generally truthful. No doubt you misunderstood her."

"No doubt."

Some years ago, when I spent a few eternal, miserable months in the service of King Cadmus, I'd known a sergeant, like myself, who claimed to know always when people lied. A centaur had galloped his way into the family lineage at some earlier point, far enough back in time to be a point of pride instead of dishonor. Whether or not that was true, Dexios had possessed an unusual ability to sniff out any soldier with either grain alcohol or a woman, two things soldiers never fail to acquire even in the midst of the Libyan Desert. Dexios would ask a few questions and could tell perpetrator from innocent by-stander much more quickly than I could. If that was centaur-blood, it did more for him than my supposedly divine blood ever had.

I was sure Meryt was lying about the stone prince. Such a story would spread among a population in less time than the plague. There had been a tone of fear in her flat denial and why would such a woman be afraid of a children's tale? Was it that fear or poverty that had sent her here. I couldn't believe in any sudden bizarre yearning to visit a muddy little town in the back of beyond.

I also felt sure that she was lying about Naunet. But why would a proud woman aid and abet a runaway daughter? Especially with a barbarian like me. I couldn't imagine a reason to for any mother to do such a thing.

My divine blood, if any, reminded me that I had a very human relative in town. If Petta knew that the Slipstone Pass was now safe, she could send a caravan over it before anyone else knew. A good profit could be made quickly.

I debated sending a message to my mother but decided against it. Why disappoint her? As soon as I wrapped up the Egyptian job, whatever it was, I'd come back. Nothing would stop me. Fjuti and Takelot had set me an example of filial devotion.

Reaching up, I lifted myself over the wall. Getting down, I sauntered off toward Petta's place. Maybe she would be grateful enough to send for that girl again. I had a long sea voyage ahead of me, after all.

CHAPTER NINE

I came back with plenty of time to spare, but the house was already stirring with last minute preparations. I saw Naunet, her arms full of linen, at the end of a hallway. She smiled and flapped her hand in a wave from beneath the pile. Then someone called to her. She smiled resignedly at me and hurried away.

The two bodyguards were already at the ship, as was Hebnetma. I was pressed into service as a strong back to load the last of the luggage into the hand-carts. Meryt kept me by her while she gave final instructions to the elderly couple who were to be caretakers until the next delegation arrived from Egypt.

"Air the rooms daily. Build fires once a week to keep the damp from damaging the plaster. You won't have to concern yourselves with any furniture except what is left in the kitchen. Be sure to sprinkle the powders I have left you around the doors and windows to keep out insects."

The old man bowed and nodded. The old woman had sharp eyes. I pitied any spider going for a stroll along her windowsills.

Meryt paused for thought, tapping with her forefinger against a small mole high on her right cheek. I hadn't noticed it in the dim light the previous night. "The money I've given you must last until the next trade commission comes. It should not be more than a year, if that. If the frogs all die, you shall have to find more. Hire a suitable boy to do it for you; I don't want you catching your death in a pond."

The old man looked confused. I translated into less scholarly words. "Frogs, yet," he said when he understood. "We don't even eat them and they keep them as pets."

"They find their noise relaxing," I explained. The old couple exchanged glances and shrugs. "They understand," I said to Meryt.

"Good. I hope they are trustworthy. The last pair tried to strip off the murals as being displeasing to some local deity or other. We had to have all the heads repainted when we came. And the local artists aren't good."

"We have some strict gods in the hills. But these are townsfolk. They probably worship at the usual temples." I asked them and the names Hera and Hephaestus came up, along with a minor local goddess. Her duties were solely concerned with domestic matters, making sure hens laid and lambs suckled, nothing to do with interior decorating. I saw no reason to mention her to Meryt.

Within an hour, I was at sea again. I would have liked a chance to question Takelot and Fjuti some more but they were in the first ship, along with their master and the captain of our little fleet. Naunet and Meryt were in the second ship, with the maidservants they'd brought along and the musicians. I could sometimes hear the music floating over the water at night.

I was in the third ship, smaller, smellier and, I felt certain, leakier than the others. My companions were the two short-statured stable hands, a grimy boy of all work, and the crew. There were no horses aboard, so the stable hands spent their time snoring in the sunshine. The boy had bad breath, pimples and a cast in one eye. Despite that, his conversation consisted solely of tales about the swathe he'd cut through the naive girls of Kalithanos. Having met some of those girls myself, I doubted his version of reality.

After about two days of this, I offered to show him a few training secrets. He was eager to learn, to build up his sunken chest and chicken-wings. I kept him at it so that he was too tired to dream of women or, indeed, anything.

If I'd had ninety days, I might have made something of him. But our voyage didn't last that long, thank the Gods. Nothing supernatural or even extra-natural like that whirlpool delayed us.

When you sail down the coast and out into the open water, the sea is a dazzling blue with unimaginable deeps growing ever darker as you float by. You know you are approaching Egypt when the blue of the water begins to mix with a milky brown, at first very pale like unbaked bread. Then as the ship travels on, the color slowly deepens, like bread in the oven as the crust begins to brown. It is the life-blood of Egypt, the Nile itself, pouring forever into the sea, carrying precious soil with it.

The other two ships looked like toys against the clear lapis blue of a twilight sky as we sailed into port. The evening had just begun to close in and before us the city of Tanis began to light her lamps. Here we would leave our deep-draft ocean-going vessels and change to the shallower draft of ships that could ply the Nile. But as we drifted past the waterfront, hearing the music and laughter from the portside houses and taverns, I wondered how we could bring ourselves to leave.

By the time the third ship had drawn up to the quayside, the formalities were over. Hebnetma stood in conversation with two men whose bearing was so haughty that they made him look like a schoolboy. He waved me over.

"This is the man of whom I spoke," he said. "Eno, these are gentlemen of the Royal Court here in Tanis."

I admit that I hardly looked my best after two weeks in a tiny ship without enough wash water. But I doubt they would have greeted me any more effusively had I been dressed in Tyrian purple with the treasure of the Indus dripping from my fingertips. I was a barbarian mercenary and thus unworthy of anything except my hire.

"Our Royal Master has given orders you are to be accommodated in the palace," one said, turning again to Hebnetma. "There will be a banquet to honor you for success with those Hittite negotiations. Pharaoh is pleased to be gracious unto you."

"My lady mother will be cast into transports of delight," the young man said. He pointedly did not say that he himself was delighted, I noticed.

After the bureaucrats had taken themselves off, I scratched my sprouting beard and asked, "What's the problem with going to the palace?"

Hebnetma stared at me as if one of the flaming torches that lit our dock had spoken. But he was just irritated enough to answer me. "I do not object to the palace. Nor even to the banquet. However, I should not be honored so. My uncle would not like it."

"Well, as you say, your mother will be pleased."

"I was being polite. As soon as she saw those men waiting for me, she claimed to be ill."

"Maybe she is."

"A most uncommonly quick-onset, then," he said dryly. "She guessed what they'd come to say and for some reason unclear to me, she wants to remain on shipboard. Impossible of course."

"Well, then, you can bet Naunet will be thrilled. Not every girl gets to stay under the roof of the Great House."

"Yes, she will be excited beyond measure. Girls are impressed by that sort of thing, I suppose. I can only hope my uncle will understand that I could not refuse without discourtesy."

That lead me to a question I'd wanted to ask for a while. "How serious is this breach between Upper and Lower Egypt?"

"There is no breach," he said loudly. Too loudly, as if other ears besides mine might be listening.

"With Lower Egypt ruled by Pharaoh's chief general and Upper ruled by the Priests of Amun? Sounds serious to me."

"You do not understand. How could you?"

"Then explain, so I don't keep making mistakes."

The porters had begun to unload the ships. Hebnetma walked away and, when I did not follow at once, hastily motioned to me to come along. He walked on a little ways, then turned abruptly into a water-side tavern. It was quiet, only a few sailors drowsing over their mugs. Hebnetma went to it like a duckling to a pond.

I followed him to a table as far from the front door as one could be in the shallow space. The lean owner brought us fresh figs, soft cheese, and honey. He also brought beer, poured in a foamy rush into stone cups.

Hebnetma lifted the filled beaker, leaned back and drank deep, the lump in his throat sliding up and down like a frog trying to escape from a jar of oil. I'd never seen a man so young drink like that. After what seemed a week, he put the beaker down and sighed from the soles of his feet.

"Drink up," he said. "You'll not find the like in all the islands of the Great Green."

Beer is the perfect drink for the Egyptians. Nothing is more refreshing during a hot day, and all the days in Egypt are hot. All the same, I had never developed much of a taste for it. The aroma, however, had a new appeal after two weeks on a ship with little but slimy water to drink. I had begun to think they'd filled their barrels from the frog-pond back in Kalithanos.

I took a few swallows to be polite and found a new enthusiasm for the brew. Nevertheless, I came after him to talk, not drink. "About what you were saying?"

He frowned and I found out why he was always at such pains to seem remote and severe. Hebnetma had one of the most expressive faces I'd ever seen. When he frowned, he looked like a baby about to cry. Telling a secret, he turned instantly into the ultimate conspirator, with squinting eyes and lips tight to his teeth. Upon tasting his first fresh food in two weeks, he transformed into a greedy child, with smacking lips and rolling eyes expressing his satisfaction. Even his nose twitched covetously. I dragged my gaze away, though I could have watched his play of expression for an hour. Any clown would have killed for a face like that, doing naturally what it took ages of training to learn.

"This looks appealing," I said, dipping the cheese in some honey.

"Fresh bread," Hebnetma ordered from the barman/owner. He nodded and stepped out his door to the bakery.

The young man leaned toward me. "I will trust you, Eno. My sister tells me that I would be wise to do so."

"She's a clever girl, your sister."

"Yes, too clever. Too clever to marry well. The man she was supposed to marry has declined. I'm sure she didn't think that would happen when she invented this ridiculous story about a ghost."

"You don't believe in ghosts?"

"Not that one," he said, expressing the vastness of his disbelief with an eyebrow that all but danced across his forehead. "But you asked me about the breakdown in our ancient ways. Many have asked why, after centuries of unification, Pharaoh should give half our country to a jumped-up nobody without past or family."

"And what is the answer?" I poured him some more beer and he drank it as eagerly as if he hadn't just sent half a gallon down his throat.

"The answer is...the will of Pharaoh. Ramesses is old, he lives now in complete seclusion, but he is still lord of this land. No one dares to question his decrees."

"How long since anyone saw him?"

"Two or three years, perhaps. All sorts of tales circulate about what he has been doing."

Some people have said that I have a nasty, suspicious mind. I suppose it may be true. "You are certain he's still alive?"

Hebnetma's dark eyes opened wide enough to distinguish the black pupil from the deep brown of his iris. "Of course he's alive. If he were dead, there would have been rites and a proclaiming of the new Pharaoh in procession from the Great Temple."

"Of course. I don't know what I could have been thinking."

As if no one ever slew a king and buried him beneath the fresh paving stones of Imhotep's New All-Night Chariot Parking.

Hebnetma tapped the back of my hand for emphasis. "Don't mention the division among people you don't know," he warned. "Officially, there is still only one Egypt, united and strong. To say otherwise is to hint that Pharaoh isn't powerful enough to hold his kingdom which is treasonous."

"It wouldn't be treason for me to say it; I'm not Egyptian."

"It would be treasonous to listen."

The barkeep had come back with the bread, still hot from the ovens. Hebnetma broke open the round loaf, inhaling the warm, yeasty aroma that arose with the steam. I had to exert strict self-command to keep from snatching it from him.

"Eat up," he said, handing me the other half. "Believe me, you won't get anything hot to eat in the palace."

"You've spent a lot of time there?"

"Not since I was a boy. My father was often there. He was a simple man, but Pharaoh was pleased to speak with him from time to time. He had a great grasp of the mood of the people and he would convey this to Pharaoh. My aunt, his sister, was attached to the Royal House as a lesser wife. I don't really remember her; she died when I was very small."

"A great honor," I said politely. But I began to recognize the signs of a man with something to say and a great reluctance to come to the point. Maybe he hadn't come here just because he was thirsty.

"Yes, it must have been. I don't remember her, really. My mother said she often complained that by the time the food came from the kitchens, it was always cold. The few times that I have gone there with my other uncle, I understood what she meant."

"This would be your uncle, the high priest?"

"Yes. Speaking of whom...."

Ah-hah! I thought.

"I know you have traveled here to serve him."

"At his request," I reminded him. I wanted that to remain perfectly clear despite the deficiency of Court Egyptian.

"As you say. But I wonder, as you are not yet in his ser...employ, whether I might hire you temporarily?"

"For what?"

He drummed his fingers on the table while he thought. "Those men weren't customs officers. They were court officials. It's not the done thing for them to meet ships, but they met ours. I'd be a fool not to wonder about that."

"What did they say?"

"The usual words about their prayers for our safe journey being answered and that Pharaoh himself took a great interest in this trade mission. Which is absurd."

"Oh?"

"It was a minor mission to an unimportant kingdom. The Hittites accepted almost my first proposal. Why should Pharaoh, why should anyone care about it? And now this banquet in my honor and orders to stay in the palace itself 'at the Sun's pleasure'."

"The Sun being Pharaoh?"

His mobile face expressed a deep cynicism that would not have been out of place on a woman in Petta's profession. "I want you to keep an eye on me for the next several days. I don't want to get taken out and lost in the desert or anything."

"Shouldn't be too tough," I said. "Keep Takelot and Fjuti close by as well. Between the three of us, we should keep anyone safe."

"I'm ordering them to watch over my mother and sister. I don't want them left vulnerable."

"What do you expect to happen?" I asked.

His fluid shrug seemed to contain all the doubt in the world. "I wish I knew. Court's a tricky place. No one speaks the truth. My mother has warned me so often about getting entrapped in the snares they weave for the unwary. I just can't think of a reason anyone in the Royal Court would take an interest in me."

When we returned to the others, I realized that Hebnetma had adopted his reserved, austere persona so that he didn't instantly give away everything he thought. I couldn't help but admire his self-discipline in controlling his eloquent features so completely.

Once out of the commercial zone, our boats were rowed past elegant villas, small compounds of several houses clustered by the water's edge, and temples, white with limestone-facing that shone in the light of the setting sun. Even this small branch of the Nile moved with impressive speed, so that our rowers had to strain against the current.

Naunet waved at me from the leading boat. I could see her lips moving as she called out something but her words were lost in the rhythmic song the boat-master played to keep his rowers in time. She said it again, making big gestures, pointing here and there. I assumed she was telling me what the buildings were as we passed them by, until her mother tugged at her clothing to make her sit down before she fell overboard. Meryt's face was rigid. She'd put on a rather thick mask of make-up and what were plainly her best jewels and robes.

Hebnetma stood at the front of that boat, still as one of the stone statues in front of a temple. His arms were folded and he swayed with the motion of the river. Takelot and Fjuti stood behind him, not nearly so steadily. Fjuti waggled his fingers at me.

The rowers pulled around a slight bend in the river. I couldn't restrain the gasp that broke from my throat at the sight before me.

The Palace of Pharaoh stood alone on a wide plain. No lesser building would be permitted to detract from the simple beauty of the site. A white wall a thousand paces long met another, ending in two tapering pylons acting as a doorway into the inner courts. A long walkway ran directly from this entrance to the river's edge where it became a pier.

Within the enclosing arms of the walls, rose a building larger than any I'd ever seen in Greece. It must have had room to house five hundred members of the court, plus all their horses and servants. Yet the place seemed eerily unoccupied. No hum of busy humanity competed with the rippling of the river. It seemed an abode for ghosts.

But the two men standing on the pier were solid enough. By the time my ship had drawn up, Hebnetma had made his bows and introduced his mother and sister. I didn't wait for the ropes to be tied. I jumped and didn't even dampen a sandal. Casually, I sauntered up to the little group.

One man was a priest, bald head gleaming where the last of the sunlight cast a thin gilding. He wore his leopard skin over one scrawny shoulder which was so sloped from scribe-work that it kept sliding off.

The other gave all the signs of an ex-soldier. He had that upright posture we teach all recruits, overlaid with the easy stance of a man who has few rivals and many followers. Though his skin was smooth like a young man's, his muscles were not as taut as once they were nor his stomach as flat, despite his evidently sucking it in. His wide-eyed gaze was fixed on Naunet, his mouth hanging slightly open. He did not hear Hebnetma speak until the boy repeated it.

"My lord," Hebnetma said as solemnly as the first time. "This is the man of whom I spoke. Eno the Thracian."

The priest looked disapproving, even moving back a little so that even my shadow did not touch him. The other man blinked as if waking from sleep then lifted a hand in stately greeting. He sized me up in a glance. "Your name precedes you, my friend. I disbelieved the tales I heard of you, for who can believe the incredible? But now that I see you, my faith is restored."

This sounded flattering. "My thanks," I said with a slight bow.

"Come," he said to Hebnetma. "A banquet has been prepared. It waits only for your ablutions. If I may beg the ladies to be swift?" He spoke to both of them, but he was looking only at Naunet. "It is long since my noon meal."

"We would not dare to keep you waiting long, my lord," Meryt said, stepping across the dock to link her arm with her daughter's. I saw the discreet pinch she gave the girl's hand, prompting her to speak. Naunet only smiled, though she might as well have shot him with an arrow.

The party walked on. I followed but first stopped to ask a question of Takelot, supervising the unloading of the baggage. "Who is that guy?"

"General Nesibanebdjedet."

"Who?"

"The next pharaoh," he said quietly. "If all the omens are correct. Most people call him Smendes."

The palace didn't diminish in grandeur as we approached. Enormous statues of gods and kings loomed up, possessed of unearthly faces and unnatural calm. The human-headed ones wore half-smiles as though their thoughts drifted through pleasant day-dreams. I recognized where Hebnetma had learned his remote and austere expressionlessness. But even his vacancy was exaggerated now that I paid more attention.

Animal-headed gods, cat, hawk, vulture, seemed immeasurably alien to me. They all had fires burning before them inn huge stone bowls. Sweet-smelling incense was replenished constantly by silent servants, fighting back the river-smell of decay. The endlessly wavering firelight imparted a semblance of life to each stone face. The sun now left only a smear of pink in the rapidly-darkening western sky - Ra gone again to his repose.

I had a disturbed feeling quite apart from my uneasiness at being watched by huge stone gods. Something was nagging at me, something wrong, even more out of place than I was.

I found myself counting the people with me. The priest. The general. An elderly man. Hebnetma. Fjuti, walking behind Naunet. Another man. Takelot watching Meryt. Another man. Three maidservants.

I looked away, out into the darkness beyond the pavement while my heart beat half a dozen strokes. Then I quickly counted again. Thirteen people. Fourteen if I were included.

Dismissing my odd disquiet as mere tiredness, and a little bit of vertigo at being on land again, I wondered why a great general would come himself to greet a rather minor functionary. Hebnetma was right in thinking this out of the ordinary.

Instead of teasing out an answer, I counted again. Thirteen persons. Fourteen persons. Thirteen.

A company of guards, very fine in matching breastplates and greaves polished to perfection, came marching out from between the pylons at the palace's front gate. They saluted briskly, row by row, clanking golden sleeves against gilded armor. They might be just for show, but their legs showed good muscle and the fists looked hard and sturdy as they struck against gleaming chests.

Smendes saw me appraising his troops. He grinned, his teeth white and strong. He was really only slightly out of condition, nothing two weeks in the field wouldn't fix. I couldn't blame him for preferring a palace even if it meant a few pouches under his dark eyes. "The men of the guard are hand-picked," he said, falling back a step to walk with me. "But not by me. I think they are all nephews of ladies in the harem."

"They show well."

"So do prize rabbits. You know as do I that muscles and marching don't make soldiers."

"But it's hard to make soldiers without them."

"True," he said, then dropped his voice. "What did he say that girl's name was?"

"Meryt?" I can never resist the urge to tease a general. It's why I never stay long in any army.

"No...the other one."

"Her name is Naunet." I tried to remember her other names, something about Harmony and Peace but I guessed he'd find out the whole thing eventually.

"Naunet. Like the goddess of the oceans. It suits her."

We were within the forecourt. It was very like the one at Kalithanos, elegant fountain, loud frogs, but on a gigantic scale. I felt as though I had shrunk by a third, which, I suppose, was the whole reason for it being that way. Anyone coming to see Pharaoh would get walloped with the knowledge that they were insignificant compared to his glory.

Here Smendes stopped. Once again his eyes went directly to Naunet's face as if he felt compelled to look at her. "I shall part from you now but not for long. Be swift and join me as soon as you may."

The ladies assured him they could be ready in the flap of a crocodile's tail and he left us.

Naunet was looking at everything, the tall tapering columns, the magnificent murals of peasants and kings alike bringing tribute, the touches of gold on painted leaves and flowers glimmering in the torchlight.

Her mother looked around as well. Meryt glanced once at me and I felt a shock. Her eyes weren't wide with wonder but with terror. Something here frightened her half-out of her wits.

One of the men escorted the ladies away, maidservants in tow. I didn't see the elderly man anymore; he must have gone ahead to warn the cooks. The other man waited to show Hebnetma and me where we'd change.

Meryt said something to her guide and came hurrying back. "A word, my son," she said. Drawing him off, she spoke to him rapidly, falling into a dialect I could not follow. But her round terrified eyes stared at nothing past his shoulder.

I turned to follow her gaze. For a moment, I saw only empty space. Then there was a shadow moving at a walking pace along the wall. A shadow of a man but no one cast it.

CHAPTER TEN

Somehow without a word or a gesture, the servant assigned to Hebnetma and me showed how earnestly he wanted us to follow him. I had no time to examine the room for spirits or to exorcise any that I might find. One did not keep even future pharaohs waiting for their supper.

He showed us into a bathing room, with long white hangings surrounding a pool of clear water. Dark blue tiles edged the water, each painted with a lotus. He clapped his hands together sharply twice and a sudden influx of young women came in answer.

The girls all carried instruments of their craft, bath brushes, unguents, combs, razors. Some were naked, their smooth brown skin gleaming. Others wore short linen shifts that left arms and legs bare. They looked at me and giggled amongst themselves. Then they swarmed.

I felt like an ostrich surrounded by chattering finches. I even have knobbly knees.

The girls were ruthlessly efficient. I was stripped and whisked into a cool tub scented with mint in a matter of seconds. The temperature chilled my reaction to the sight of those beautiful creatures, mostly clad in transparent, clinging wet linen. I kept my eyes closed most of the time for safety's sake. If only they didn't tickle so.

Hebnetma, more used to their ministrations, was wise enough not to struggle when they plunged his head under water. I got a snoutful and came up snorting like a whale with a head cold. They laughed, dunked me again, and swooped in to shave my face. Quickly, my chin was smoother than it had been since I was twelve.

They wanted to shave other things as well but I fought them off. Efficiency is all very well, but there are some things a man would rather have left in a natural, disorganized condition. They pouted but gave me my own way.

Dressed in a long formal tunic, faultlessly shaved, Hebnetma looked like he'd just stepped off the painted wall behind him. A girl was drawing careful lines around his eyes but he looked at me and laughed so hard at my attempts to communicate my wish to keep my balls unshaved that she had to wipe off the kohl and start over.

The chamberlain returned, carrying a tunic over his arm. He held it up, looking from it to me. Even I could see that it was going to be far too short for decency. He snapped his fingers and another servant ran in with more white linen bundled against his chest. I shook off the water-logged girls, who seemed reluctant to let me out of the tub, and stepped up onto the tessellated floor.

I towered over all of them. The chamberlain cast an appraising glance over my body. Then, in one sudden movement, he yanked down one of the hangings around the pool. He tossed the length to the other servant who sighed and bowed.

A quick rip to create an opening for my head to go through and I was dressed for dinner.

Hebnetma bit his fist to keep his laughter from spoiling his make-up any further. The girls didn't bother to conceal their giggles and witticisms as they fluttered around me, rapidly pleating the curtain and tying a sash tightly around my waist to hold the multitude of tiny pleats in place. They concealed the fact that it was wide open on both sides. I hoped the dining room wouldn't be breezy.

"You look well," Hebnetma declared, compelling the chamberlain to concur. You would think a court servant could lie better than that.

I thanked him anyway. "A most ingenious solution to the difficulty."

"Your own sandals will be returned to you shortly," he said. "Alas that we have none worthy of so great a foot."

All my gear had been taken away to be polished, pressed or shined. All except my sword-in-scabbard which I had not surrendered to the pretty hand that had tried to take it. I went now and picked it up. The chamberlain and Hebnetma exchanged glances, alarmed at this potential crime against etiquette.

"Eno," Hebnetma began.

I handed the sword to the chamberlain. He flinched but took it. "Keep it handy for me."

"If you would like to keep it within reach of your mighty arm, lord, I can convey it to the table for you."

"I won't need it, will I? You have small knives with which I may cut my meat?"

"Of course, lord."

"Then hang on to it or put it where I'll sleep. And treat it well," I said. "It came from the hand of a god."

The man bowed deeply and carried it away at arm's length as if it might turn and bite him. Hebnetma grinned at me. "A good tale. Servants are a superstitious lot. He won't dare draw it or let anyone else do so."

"I wish it were just a tale. It really is not of human manufacture, so far as I know."

His eyebrows doubted me. But I was a guest and must be humored. "Come," he said. "We lack but one thing for a dinner of this importance."

This time, he clapped his hands. In hustled a parade of girls each holding what seemed to be, at first glance, decapitated heads. I fought down my nausea and realized they were just wig stands, though painted in life-like colors.

"You must choose first, as my guest," Hebnetma said.

They ranged from a full-bottomed wig with long oiled curls to a frisky little arrangement of braids looped up into swirls. I ran my hand over my head, the close-cropped hair pricking my palm, and refused politely.

Heb, his own head shining, obviously thought this was merely low-brow squeamishness. Highly civilized people do just as many things that barbarians find disgusting as the reverse. "They aren't uncomfortable," he hastened to say. "They don't even itch much, once you get used to it."

I pictured myself, square-jawed and round-headed, peering coquettishly through long black curls or balancing a small bath-mat on top of my head. Politely but firmly, I insisted that I would be more comfortable without a wig.

Hebnetma chose one that in all respects seemed identical to the one he wore every day. But he exclaimed over it, smoothing the braids with little appreciative noises. "So fine," he said. "Smell that?" He waved the hairpiece at me. "Myrrh."

The girls helped him to set it on his head properly.

"It is time, gentlemen," the chamberlain said, returning. He seemed more wary of me than before.

His courtesy lacked the slight tinge of condescension I'd noted earlier.

We met Naunet and Meryt emerging from their chamber. Still ushered, we entered the main chamber at the same instant that Smendes' group appeared at the far end.

"There you are, Eno," he said heartily. "I hope you have brought your appetite from the Great Green."

"I've been hungry for a week," I said. "Shipboard fare has never agreed with me."

"I get sea-sick myself. It's why I preferred the army."

His entourage laughed after the pause that the jokes of all great men receive.

Smendes came over to meet us. He snapped his fingers and two servants knelt on the floor, opening small chests. "In honor of your visit, Meryt, may I offer you and...your daughter these gifts?"

Meryt looked surprised and forced a smile. She still looked frightened. "Oh, my, I didn't...thank you, my lord. You are too generous."

"It is nothing."

She held her wrist out, turning it this way and that to admire a cuff bracelet inset with a medallion of some kind, perhaps a scarab beetle for good luck or an ankh for long life.

Smendes reached into the casket and brought out two gem-encrusted bands, about as wide as my thumb is long. The colors flashed in the torchlight, red, purple, blue, and the gleam of gold spacers and clasps. Stylized claws dangled from the gemstone beads.

He knelt before Naunet, his back straight, and looked up into her face. He reached out toward her foot without touching it. "Anklets, to grace what needs no adornment."

Naunet glanced shyly at the courtiers standing around, surprised and knowing looks on all their over-fed faces. Her mother's pleasure in her gift seemed to vanish in a little puff of smoke. She took a step forward as if to protest but I was in the way. Meryt caught my eye and her protest went unspoken. Hebnetma, as always, remained impassive.

Sliding her foot forward, Naunet said, "It is not seemly, my lord, for you to fasten them on."

"No one else shall," he said, his voice low enough only to reach her ears and mine. I doubt even Meryt caught the deep, passionate feeling behind the words. I foresaw trouble ahead. Maybe oracularity is catching.

"They belonged to my mother," he announced, rising to his feet after fastening one about each of her slim ankles. "She would be pleased to know they have passed to one so lovely and pure of spirit." There was a smattering of applause.

We were all shown to an enclosed terrace at the far end of the main chamber. Roofed with cedar, it looked out toward the river. A few musicians played a haunting tune on pipes and harps.

The soft blue of the evening sky was still tinged with the glowing light of the sun's setting. Sweet-smelling torches lit the space and young boys with large palm-leaf fans stirred the air to spread the scent and to keep off flies. At the far end there was a large table, loaded with fruits, what looked like half a roasted bull, some birds still in their feathers, and loaves of bread both leavened and unleavened. Everything was displayed with elegance and care, as though to create a picture as mouthwatering as the meal itself.

We were shown to our seats, small tables beside us, and the servants began to bring our meals. At first, being hungry, I had no leisure to observe anything. But I noticed that when I lifted the last piece but one of bread to my lips, a servant was already there to replenish my plate. As I lifted my goblet for the last sip it held, someone would be there to pour for me before I put the goblet down.

I began to realize just how well-organized this palace was.

Though Meryt and her daughter were the only female guests, they seemed utterly at ease. No Greek woman, unless of the courtesan class, would ever eat openly with men not of their family.

Naunet sat beside me, showing me how to eat properly the delicacies laid before us. I'd been to Egypt before but had never been entertained on this scale. Naunet demonstrated proper form without making me feel either clumsy, though I was, or barbarous, though I am.

As I navigated my way through a serving of bony little birds, I noticed her vivacity had dimmed. "Is anything wrong?"

"He keeps staring at me," she murmured, leaning forward so that her hair covered her cheek.

"Who?"

"The general."

I glanced at him. Smendes was reaching for his wine yet I got the impression that he'd only just turned his head away. The faience beads in his wig were still swinging.

"You do look nice," I said to Naunet. A wide collar of linen embroidered with beaded lotus flowers encircled her brown throat, making it appear almost too slender to support her head. Earrings in the shape of lapis leopards played hide-and-seek among her curls. "He's probably never seen such a pretty girl."

She scoffed even as she blushed. "And the women's quarters crammed with beauties from every town in the Two Lands!"

"But they all belong to Pharaoh, don't they? Poor Smendes never gets so much as a hand to hold."

"Don't you mind if he stares at me and gives me presents?" She poked out one foot from beneath her gown. "They're very pretty. And far too valuable for a mere nobody."

I'd forgotten that I was supposed to be her future husband, according to prophecy. Naunet was a good, brave, dear girl but I wished Smendes all the luck in the world. "I'm a guest in this house," I temporized. "I can't very well pick a quarrel with the man any more than you can throw those anklets in his face."

"No, I suppose not."

"Besides, he seems like a pleasant enough fellow. Just in the prime of life, not bad-looking, good prospects."

"You sound like a marketplace matchmaker." Still, she glanced shyly at Smendes. "It's hard to tell."

"What is?"

"What someone is really like. A man might look like a young god, strong, round-limbed, and brave, yet prove a broken reed when the waters of trouble arise."

Remembering the young man who had broken off their betrothal, I wanted to pat her shoulder or hand comfortingly. But not with Smendes watching.

Giving powerful men cause to resent me is always worth avoiding.

"It's just like anything else," I said. "It pays to wait for the best."

Naunet shook back her braids and gave me a wide, mocking smile. "Not every man is like you, Eno."

"I know I will regret asking...what am I?"

"Uncomplicated."

I suppose no man likes to think of himself as easy to understand. We all like to pretend to have uncharted depths, the possessors of unplumbed souls containing mysteries too rare to be shared with every Theon, Deke, and Homer.

Yet I laughed because she was right. "Oh, I'm uncomplicated enough all right. But somehow my life never is."

"I didn't mean to hurt your feelings."

"I'm not insulted. You are too young to be so cynical, however."

"I don't think I'll ever believe anything a man tells me from now on. I've learned a lot just lately." She glanced at me and her eyes were shimmering with tears. "My mother received a message from my betrothed's father. Our marriage has been refused, irrevocably."

"I thought...your brother seemed to think it was already decided that you wouldn't marry that guy."

"They never said for certain. I thought, maybe there was still a chance." She sniffed delicately.

I noticed that Smendes had become ever more interested in watching us. As Naunet caught a tear on the back of her finger, he rose and approached my table. A furrow had appeared between his brows. He carried his hands clenched, his body tight.

Nudging the girl seemingly by accident with my elbow, I pasted a smile of welcome on my face. "A delightful meal, general. I always say there's no place like Egypt for real hospitality!"

He ignored me. "The moon is rising, if Lady Naunet would care to watch it in my company."

"Indeed, I should be most pleased to do so. If you will pardon me, Eno?"

"By all means. I'll just have another cup of wine. Moon gazing is for the romantic at heart, not old campaigners like me."

In the end, we all shuffled outside to a pavement running alongside the ever-moving Nile to watch the moon ascend, even the musicians. If Smendes had hoped to get Naunet to himself, neither her mother nor any member of his entourage seemed likely to permit it. As is often the case with a rising star, many lesser comets will chase it wherever it goes.

I got pushed to the rear of the group, happily. I wanted to observe whether or not the 'ghost' would reappear among this group. The figure I'd glimpsed earlier had been hawk-nosed, elderly, and thin-shanked. He hadn't worn a wig, only his own scanty, grey hair. I started to count how many people were present but they were all shifting around, trying to get a better view. I started to work my way around the perimeter of the pavement, hoping to see faces instead of backs.

They all gasped as the light suddenly grew much stronger. I turned and stood, like the rest, open-mouthed.

I've seen the moon rise often at sea and have been amazed by the size and grandeur of that silver disk, rising as though on a pillar of its own light. I have seen it in the mountains, where it looked near enough to pluck from the sky. I've seen it gold as a king's treasure and cold as a queen's heart. I had never seen it burning a fiery scarlet until that night. It was as though it had been dipped in heart's blood and spread it by reflection over the Nile.

"It's a bad omen," someone murmured.

"Consult the oracle," someone else said, not, surprisingly enough, Naunet.

"Yes, that is wise," Smendes said. "Return to your plates, my friends. I will go at once to speak with the oracle. Eno, will you accompany me?"

"With pleasure. Is it far?" It was fairly obvious that he didn't want me return to my heart-to-heart talk with Naunet.

"No, he lives nearby."

I wished I had a moment to grab my sword but Smendes was already walking away. One of those instant decision commanders.

With a sharp jerk of my head, I told Hebnetma to go back to the tables. Hopefully, he would stay put until I came back. He should be safe enough.

Meryt put her arm around her daughter to guide her back to the terrace. She seemed to have quite a bit to say. I wasn't sure I trusted Meryt in all ways, though I felt fairly certain that she wasn't the sort to scold a girl for disobeying the dictates of propriety. Naunet had told me her mother had approved of her following me into the hills. Meryt had denied it. Of the two, I believed Naunet. A strange thing for a mother to encourage shamelessness in a daughter.

I cast one glance back to the pavement as I hastened after Smendes. An old man stood there, hawk-nosed and so frail the red moonlight shone through him. His fathomless eyes followed me then turned as though under compulsion after Naunet. Even as I watched, he faded from view.

Tripping over the unraveling hem of my improvised garment, it was only by a last second twist that I kept myself from falling into the Nile. I heard a sighing hiss and watched as crocodiles slipped, one by one, into the water.

If it came to a choice between ghosts and crocodiles, I'd take the man-eaters. Those I could at least wrestle.

Catching up with the general, I asked him what he thought the red moon meant.

"Nothing, probably. Not everything is an omen, bad or good. I got over believing in omens after my first battle." He eyed me. "I take it that you aren't superstitious either. Greeks usually aren't."

"You know many Greeks? But no. I'm not Greek and I'm not superstitious." I wondered what he'd say if I told him the reason. When you've met a god or two face-to-face, you don't have to spit in your hand for luck or spill wine on the ground in libation. But you'd be damned stupid not to.

"The sunset was quite red, too," I added. "That might have been the explanation for the moon to look like that."

He turned and looked at it again, resting above a fan of closely-planted palms. "It seems to be passing off. Khonsu is himself again."

This took me aback. I'd forgotten for the moment that, in Egypt, the personification of the moon is a god. I wondered how Artemis, our lunar goddess in her form as Selene, felt about that. "Or only faintly pink," I added.

"Nevertheless, we will seek out the oracle." He pushed open a small, inconspicuous door lost among shadows. By my reckoning, we were about as close to the extreme back of the palace as one could get. Some refuse had been piled here, broken furniture, a cracked amphora or two, a couple of head-rests with snapped supports.

"Not a very grand place for a seer," I said. "Most of 'em make a bigger show of their powers."

"This one doesn't have to. Besides, he likes to fiddle with repairing such things when he has the time. Mended my favorite wine-cup so you can't even see the crack." He turned in the opening. "Will you wait here to guard this entrance?"

"Take your time," I said, more sure than ever that he had simply wanted to break up my intimate conversation with Naunet. I'd fallen in love at first sight myself once upon a time. Irrational jealousy is a well-known side effect.

I took a turn up and down the garden while waiting for him to return. A few night birds called beyond the palace wall. I heard a little music start up somewhere out there as well, a lonely flute keeping someone company. With the cooling of the day, the strong smells of dust and the river faded so that the scent of flowers could dominate. I hoped the oracle would tell Smendes that a red moon meant he'd soon be happily married to a girl he'd just met.

Hearing footsteps approaching, I edged back toward the rear entrance to the palace. Smendes wasn't paying me but I wouldn't really let him be assassinated, not when he boded well to take Naunet's mind off me.

I found a good-sized patch of shadow and stood in it, hardly breathing, wishing I wasn't wearing white.

For a moment, the breeze died. I saw him clearly, an old man, hawk-nosed, dark eyes fixed upon the ground. The moonlight rendered him pale as the linen kilt he wore. He paused and looked right at me.

I jumped out and grabbed him. The plate he carried in his hand went flying, bouncing off a palm-tree. The arm in my hand was scrawny, tough, and entirely material. He wore a gold ring that reflected the moonlight, an oval cartouche that covered his forefinger from knuckle to last joint. I don't read Egyptian hieroglyphs but I didn't have to. Only royals wear a ring like that.

CHAPTER ELEVEN

"That was my dinner," he said, quite mildly, all things considered.

I'd let go of him fast. The penalty for grabbing a pharaoh must be pretty steep. This wasn't just a king; to his people, he was God-on-earth.

"I apologize. I thought you were a ghost."

His thin eyebrows rose. "Indeed? How fascinating. Why did you think so?"

"Because I saw one."

"Are you a magician, then? Or a priest?"

"No, I'm just a hero for hire. My name's Eno the Thracian."

"Ah." He brushed off the side of his kilt where there was a slight smear. "You are a visitor to this land, then."

"That's right." It occurred to me, belatedly, that it was odd that the Lord of the Two Lands would be fetching his own supper. The least I could do was offer to get him some more.

"No, I thank you. I was not very hungry. Come, and tell me more about your ghost."

I followed him inside. He picked up an oil-lamp from a table and lit it at another. Carrying it before him, he led me deeper into this side of the palace. Like the exterior, it lacked the grandeur to be found at the front. The furnishings were sparse even by Egyptian standards and shabby. The room we entered had one chair, a bedstead, and a washstand with a battered bowl and vessel.

A few ordinary statues of gods stood on a shelf, hawk-headed Horus, protector of the royal house, lion-lady Sekhmet, goddess of war, and beaky ibis-headed Thoth, god of knowledge. A few flowers were laid by their feet in offering. The statues weren't grand, golden or gem-laden. They were simple and somewhat gaudily painted. You could pick up their twin at any common marketplace or find similar representations in any basic house in the land.

Everywhere else were reed-baskets, piled to overflowing with scrolls and clay-tablets. Rolls spilled from under the raised bed frame, tumbled from corners, sprouted from under other baskets.

Pharaoh waved me to the only chair and seated himself, scrawny brown legs dangling, on the bed. He studied me for a long moment. "Now, about this ghost of yours."

"He's not mine. My ghosts stay quietly in the past."

"You are fortunate," he said dryly. "Please go on."

Though I'm no blabber-mouth, something about his very stillness drew words from me until I'd told him everything from the time I arrived in Kalithanos until this evening. But even as I spoke, my curiosity grew.

Why would the master of at least half of Egypt, famous for wealth and power, live in this small room at the back of his own palace? Why did he have no servants, guards, or women to tend him? What was he studying among all these scrolls, of both Egyptian and foreign manufacture? I saw hieratic, which is basically hieroglyphic shorthand, Greek writing, both recent and some seriously archaic, incised cuneiform on tablets from the desert kingdoms to the east, and other things I couldn't even tell if they were words or merely what was left when you dipped an earthworm in ink and let him roam.

When I reached the end of my tale, he hopped off the bed and reached behind a basket for a cup and a beaker. "Have a bit of this. It's a cordial my stomach and bowel physician brews up. Not untasty, though it hasn't done a thing for my stomach or bowels."

"Wormwood, fenugreek, and caraway mulled in wine?" I asked after sipping it gingerly.

"Are you a physician too?"

"Only of battle-wounds and blisters."

"Ah, then you have been a soldier. I led my armies in war several times but I would not say I'd ever been a soldier."

I liked him. He might have been a god-king but he was also a gentleman. "What are you studying?" I asked, looking around at the papyri everywhere.

He smiled sadly. "Nothing now. Some years ago, I considered attempting a history of my people and my reign. I began it once or twice but lost my way among the pages. It is too great a task now for me."

I remembered that this was a man who had lost many sons. I could imagine taking refuge from such grief in the exploits of my ancestors, if I had any worthy of the name. "That's too bad. I bet it would have been interesting. Kings don't usually write their own histories."

"You know who I am, then?"

I pointed to his ring. "That gave it away."

He rubbed his thumb over the gold oval. "Force of habit," he said. "I haven't removed this ring in forty years, since my father put it on my finger the day he told me I was to inherit his throne and his kingdom. A poor job I have made of it since then."

"I don't know...."

"Oh, do not flatter me, Eno. My father would not have divided the kingdom, nor would he hand his power over to an upstart general of no particular family."

"You mean Smendes?"

"So they call him now. He will take another name some day in the not-too-distant future. A throne name, like mine. It is to be hoped he will not choose to be another Ramesses. There have been too many of us."

"But they call you Ramesses the Great," I said.

His laughter ended in a rattling choke. I wondered if the cough and lung physician had seen him recently. "All kings are called 'great' until they die. Few enough support the title afterwards."

He poured out some cordial for himself and knocked it back like an old salt in a seaside tavern. His wrinkled old eyes studied me. "You have told me a strange tale indeed. I wonder how much of it I believe."

Laughing again at my insulted expression, he tipped out another drink. "You must realize that I have heard many tales. All from those who would, one way or another, sway me to their side. It would be easier to believe that you are an assassin, sent by Smendes, or another, to hasten my end. Are you?"

"No."

"You have no protest to make?"

"I don't take those kinds of jobs. I'm a hero, not a murderer."

"I believe you. You have pride, but it is not the kind of cold pride that makes an assassin."

He stood up. "Very well. It won't be long before my courtiers retire for the night. If you and I stand watch outside this maiden's chamber, we may be able to see this ghost. If we do, I will know that what you have said is the truth."

"I hope he shows up. But he faded out right in front of me. I couldn't be mistaken."

"You are a man who mingles with gods. Why should you cavil at a spirit?"

"Maybe Apollo gave me this sight. If so, I don't want to see any more of them."

"You are fortunate. I see many ghosts. Some do not even know they are no longer among the living." He clapped a hand on my knee. "Come, my friend, if I may call you so on such short acquaintance. We will seek this one out."

It was easy to forget that Ramesses was the mightiest ruler in the world today. He'd forgotten it so thoroughly himself that not even his own servants looked twice at him as he led me through the halls of his palace. He was more humbly dressed than the boy who carried away the nightsoil, as brown as the laborer who threshed his grain, and thin as the poorest of the poor. Yet his eyes were as sharp as his profile and his dignity so innate that it shone all the stronger for the simplicity and poverty of his appearance.

The major-domo who had aided Hebnetma and me earlier in the evening came trotting over. "There you are," he said to me. "Your companions were seeking you. They have retired."

He glanced at Ramesses without curiosity. "Were you showing him the way? That was well-done but you may go about your other duties now."

Ramesses bowed. "It is no trouble. You have many important duties to attend to."

The servant raised his brows at hearing perfect Court Egyptian on the lips of someone who looked like a gardener. "By the way," I said. "Could I have my sword back now?"

"If you really require it..."

"I do indeed. Just run along and get it for me."

He wanted to protest, I could tell, at the breakdown in protocol. The first rule in a good butler's handbook is 'always endeavor to disarm barbarians'. I leaned forward a little, looming, one might say, and he hurried off.

"Why didn't he know you?" I asked in a whisper.

"Why should he? Pharaohs wear the glorious double-crown and false beard of electrum and enamel. They carry a crook and a flail as symbols of their might. They can hardly move for the weight of a vast gold pectoral and walk in gold sandals. I am an old man who wears only a soft, faded kilt and sandals of palm. I cannot, therefore, be Pharaoh."

"Which one is the disguise?" I asked.

"I knew when I was young. I have forgotten now."

The servant came back, my sword wrapped in a shroud of linen. I buckled the belt on, gave him back his linen, and sent him away again. For the first time since my bath, I felt like myself again, long linen dress or no. Realizing my shoulders had been stuck in a dignified hunch for a couple of hours, I stretched, feeling the tension of forced civility falling away.

"Come," Ramesses said, "the women's quarters are this way."

"Will she be there?"

"Almost certainly. My ladies would not miss a chance to ask a thousand questions about the world beyond Egypt. Most of them hardly believe there is such a place."

"Sometimes I wonder. Your palace keeps early hours," I said, passing through the empty, echoing halls.

"We are a desert people. The sun is more than our god, it is our clock, our taskmaster, our punishment and our joy. Besides, there are many dangers in our desert at night. The scorpion, the lion, the demons. Our souls are always in peril in the night."

"I'll be careful. Not that the daytime has ever been all that much more safe for me."

"Ah, you are a hero. Safety is not for such as you."

The guards at the door were not Takelot and Fjuti, though they might have looked much the same after ten years of bountiful meals and daily massages. Their arms were like pillars and their legs like the pylons that supported the palace wall. Every inch of their ebony bodies gleamed with expensive oils.

Ramesses walked up as though they weren't even there. They let him pass but blocked me with one arm. "It's all right," Ramesses said. "Lady Aimut sent for me. There's a scorpion loose in the Chamber of Morning. I'm the Royal Remover of Small Pests."

"Who's he then?" one of the guards asked in a voice like the depths of the sea.

"He's my assistant. He holds the bag. He can wait here if one of you would like to help me."

They looked at each other measuringly. "I don't like scorpions," the guard said. "I was stung once when I was little."

"Me either," said the other. "Hate 'em. What's the sword for?" he asked me.

"I don't like scorpions either. So sometimes I sting back."

The first guard nodded at Ramesses. "All right then. Be quick about it. We go off shift in a bit."

The women inside knew their lord for who he was. The ones who were still awake gathered around us. They were not the sinuous beauties that Naunet and I had imagined. These were sober, middle-aged women with soft bodies and kindly faces.

One, with striking bands of silver in her hair, bowed before him and asked, "How may we serve my lord?"

"Lady Aimut, one of my senior wives," Ramesses said in an aside to me. "Where is the girl Naunet and her mother?"

"The girl sleeps in the Chamber of Youthful Repose. It was pleasant to decorate it again."

"As in the days of our youth? We took little repose as I recall."

She basked in his smile and her happiness was reflected in the other faces. I remembered that some of these women must have given him the sons that were now lost. He may have retreated from this world, through grief or weariness, but their lives were still bound up with his. Now he came among them again, only to ask them about some other women. I felt ashamed.

"And the mother?"

"She played senet with us for a while. Alas, she drank too deeply of the honeyed wine. We made her comfortable on a couch in my chamber."

"You have done rightly."

She bowed again, her arms crossed over her chest. The others followed suit, like sheaves of wheat bending to the wind.

"We wish to keep watch over the girl," Ramesses said. "This man fears a demon or malignant spirit wishes to harm her."

They muttered in surprise and looked openly at me for the first time. One or two smiled shyly, mistaking me perhaps for an anxious lover. Lady Aimut lead us deeper into the women's quarters, past sleeping alcoves and bathrooms. I heard some snoring.

Naunet's room was garlanded with flowers that, only upon closer inspection, proved to be mosaics of faience tiles. "It is the bridal chamber," Ramesses said. Lady Aimut smiled again at memories.

She motioned for us to wait outside and stepped softly into the room, her feet bare. After a moment, she returned. "She sleeps soundly, as the young do. I think if you were to seat yourselves within and make no noise, she would not awaken."

Like most Egyptian beds, Naunet's was raised a foot or so off the ground to keep vermin at bay. Soft white curtains hung around her sleeping form, while a bowl of incense smoldered in the only window, high up in the wall, safeguard against gnats and mosquitoes.

I motioned Ramesses toward the only stool and went myself to the window to sit on the floor beneath it. Lady Aimut watched us, then quietly slipped away.

Outside, I heard some frogs croaking and, far away, the howl of some hunting animal. I also heard the crunch of gravel beneath heavy footsteps. Someone stumbled and I heard a familiar voice say, "Set take these stones!"

With a jump onto the wall and a simultaneous grab of the window's base, I raised myself up and hissed into the night. "Fjuti? Is that you?"

"Oh, hey, Eno," he said cheerfully, waving at me some three feet above his head. The moon illuminated my face. I hushed him, glancing over my shoulder at the bed. The girl didn't twitch.

"Are you guarding Naunet?" I asked.

"That's right. Her brother's nervous. You guarding her too, huh?"

"Where's Takelot?"

"He's guarding Mr. Hebnetma. Since you kind of disappeared for a while."

"Yeah, I was unavoidably detained. Look, I'm going to be watching here from the inside so you can go join your cousin. I'll make everything right with your boss in the morning."

"Oh, sure. Whatever you think is best. You know he's planning to head out as soon as possible tomorrow? I don't know why he's in such a hurry. This is a great place. Love the food."

"His uncle is waiting for him to come home."

"Yeah, our mothers too. See you later, Eno."

The desert had cooled rapidly once the sun had withdrawn. Mist had gathered in the corners of the garden, laying across the pathways, swirling as Fjuti passed. The moon had risen above all this, shining brightly into the window. I stayed an extra moment, admiring the peaceful scene. The frogs had recommenced singing.

Even if I had known that somewhere under that moon a young man ran for his very life, his mouth too dry to scream, his heart bursting from his side, I couldn't have saved him. I have to remind myself of that from time to time. I could not have saved any of them.

I let myself down from the window, dropping softly to the ground. The moon shone in through the window, highlighting the still figure on the bed.

Ramesses had moved from his seat to stand beside Naunet's head. He swayed slightly, a reed troubled by the current. His eyes looked huge, hollow and black in the pallid light, the shadows in his cheeks like cuts.

I said something commonplace to him. Ramesses answered, only his voice came from a different part of the room. He rose now from his seat. "Stay where you are. I will speak to him."

The figure by the bed turned at Ramesses' voice. It seemed to waver like the heated air above a flame. Ramesses came neared, gazing in amazement, sweat pouring down his face.

In profile, they were astonishingly alike. High-ridged noses, deep-set eyes, the same angles of brow and chin mirrored one another.

"Tell me, oh my father, why have you sent this, your *ka*, forth into this house which once you ruled."

"Father?" I muttered.

Ramesses showed me his palm, enjoining my silence. "Speak, oh my father. What have I, your miserable son, done or left undone? In what way have I failed in my duty to you, living or dead? If the beer and bread I leave at your tomb is insufficient, I vow to double it." Bowing in abject humility, as the lowliest peasant would bow to the mightiest Pharaoh, he waited for the spirit to speak.

But he only turned again toward Naunet. Ramesses' voice had been so low that she'd never stirred. Now, however, she moved restlessly on her carved headrest, clutching her single sheet to her chest.

"I don't think it's got anything to do with you," I said, braving Ramesses' anger. "This is about Naunet."

The ghost flicked those bottomless eyes toward me. "Yes," he said. His voice seemed to come from infinitely far away, like the echo of an echo whispered on the other side of the world.

"The girl?" Ramesses stepped up to the edge of the bed. He looked down at her, gasped, and looked again, his eyes wide. "Who is she?" he asked me.

I told him all I knew, which wasn't much. "Maybe he knows more."

Already fading, the ghost shook its head.

"Wait," Ramesses demanded. "Father...my sons. What ails this land that my sons should be lost to me thus?"

For an instant, the ghost solidified, looking at Ramesses with infinite compassion. "Cursed...."

"Cursed? By who? For what crime?"

"Cursed...."

"I beseech you, Father, go to the Lord Osiris there in the Lands Beyond and beg him to intercede for my sons so that your legacy will not be lost to the sands."

"Yes."

With that, the ghost of Ramesses' father faded into mist and silence. Ramesses himself had sunk onto his knees, weeping helplessly. All his attempts to distance himself from life, from caring, had crashed in upon him.

"There's no escape," he said, through his sobs. "I see that now. Living or dead, we are bound to this world forever."

I tried to help him to rise. He was as limp as wet papyrus. He dug his fingers into my arm. "Who in this life will honor my name and feed my *ka*? All my sons but three are dead and they may not live another span of hours. I will be a starving ghost...and all my ancestors will starve along with me."

Naunet coughed and sat up slowly. The sheet that covered her slid down, showing that she slept naked according to her people's custom. "Eno?" she said, rubbing one eye with the palm of her hand.

She saw I was not alone and let out a little screech, scrabbling for the sheet. "Oh, who is that?"

Beyond the window, beyond the palace wall, beyond the river, came another scream as if in answer. It shook the very air. A man's scream, on a rising scale of utmost terror, that awoke an equal fear in everyone who heard it. Even Ramesses forgot his grief and froze in horror.

I let go of him and bounded again to the wall. I pushed myself through the small window, leaving behind some patches of skin and a broken incense bowl.

I saw someone running flat out for the river, breaking through muddy banks. He stumbled out into the water up to his knees. I shouted, "Go back...the crocodiles!" I could tell he heard me by his hesitation. He shook his head and came on.

I jumped down, leapt the wall in a bound and a scramble of toes and fingers, and ran toward the point where he'd emerge, if he emerged at all. I could hear him splashing, at least, I hoped it was him. What could be behind him so horrible that he'd risk crocodiles rather than face it?

"I'm coming!" I shouted.

Then another shriek split the night, only to end abruptly. I heard a huge splash. Then only silence.

CHAPTER TWELVE

By the time I emerged from the tangled reeds, it was too late. Rings spread out to touch the bank at my feet. The bizarre curse on the sons of Ramesses had struck at its latest victim.

I swam across the Nile, almost wishing a crocodile would try it as I was angry enough to bite back. Nothing stirred in the dark water.

Pulling myself up onto the bank, I heard a low growling off to my right, a deep animal thrumming that played upon my tense feelings like a harpist upon her instrument. I drew my sword, shaking off the water drops, bright in the moonlight, while I pawed the mud off my face. "Who's there?" I called futilely.

I didn't heard anything further but an odor came to me, stronger than the decayed smell of the river mud, a rich stink like an army latrine ditch on a hot summer's day. It reminded me of something I'd smelled recently and long ago as well. Catching a stronger whiff of the scent in the back of my throat, I gagged, wishing I hadn't eaten so much at dinner.

Slashing through the cattails, I made my way to where I'd last seen the man standing on the edge of the riverbank. The moonlight shone nearly as bright as day, showing me his footprints. He'd run on the balls of his feet, slipping and sliding, blurring the prints. He'd stopped in a small clear spot, where the reeds had been dug up by some large animal. I didn't know what a hippopotamus' footprints looked like. It must have been something just as large and heavy that had torn up the ground.

My man's prints were confused, superimposed over the animal tracks. He'd paced several steps in either direction, afraid of the river and yet more afraid of whatever had stalked him. I would have liked to have found out how far and long he'd been running but the ground became both dusty and hard a bare hundred yards away from the Nile. Some swirl of current had kept this year's Inundation from laying silt to this part of the land.

He'd chosen the river. The prints went up to the very edge, deeper where he'd steadied himself to dive in. Then he'd turned to face the other way. Had it been my shout that turned him back?

I could see by the shadows on the edges that his prints had suddenly become very much deeper. He'd taken one step forward, his legs apart, and had sunk in. I wasn't leaving footprints that deep standing on the same patch of ground yet the man I'd seen had been almost boyishly slight of build.

I turned again to the river. He'd stood her, nearly all his weight on that back leg. I couldn't understand at first why the heel was sunk so deep in the rich black mud that it seemed impossible that he was not still stuck here.

Mimicking what must have been his last movements, I realized that he'd fallen backwards into the water. That explained the great splash I'd heard before I crossed over.

I waded in, feeling with my feet for anything out of the ordinary. The water was neither deep nor swift here, though I could not see down into it. Crouching, I waved my hands through the water until my questing fingers touched the bend of an up-flung arm, an arm that did not give way like flesh but remained as immobile as stone.

Slipping under the surface, sliding in the muck, I heaved him onto the bank. He landed rocking on his back. As I dragged myself out, I heard shouts and saw lights darting over the water. The shrieks had roused the palace and Ramesses had mustered his guard into flat-bottomed skiffs. I shouted and they altered course to find me.

I stood there, dripping, feeling an upwelling of sorrow for the old man. Two sons left and where were they? Already stone figures in some desert landscape?

Takelot and Fjuti jumped out, carrying torches above their heads, the flames pale in the clear moonlight. Ramesses stepped onto the bank, his body tensed in preparation for the blow to come.

He took a torch and leaned down close to the still and pitiful figure. The firelight gave the illusion of motion to the golden stone. Though the boy's body was contorted, his face agape with horror, every detail of his form was as crisp as if chiseled by a master sculptor.

"Yes, this is my son, Kemes."

"Are you sure, sire?" Smendes asked, stepping ashore from the second boat.

"It is given to me to recognize all my children, no matter how much time has passed or ch-changed they may be."

He stood up right slowly, not nearly so straight-backed as before. "Let him be taken reverently from this place. He will join his brothers in the secret tomb in the hills."

Tears slipped between the deep lines on his face. My own eyes pricked. "Go with Smendes, Eno, my friend. We will speak again at sunrise. I have not the strength now." I bowed with the others as he entered a boat to return to his palace. I knew he'd hear the boy's footstep in every room.

Smendes waited until he was well-out into the current before giving his orders, short sharp instructions for the carrying away of young Kemes. He also ordered a complete search of the area. The guards spread out. Smendes paused beside the 'statue'. I saw him pat it awkwardly on the twisted shoulder, a gruff soldier offering awkward comfort to a fallen comrade.

I motioned to Fjuti, who stepped over to me. I turned away from the general so my words would not carry to him. "When you are done here, attend on me with your cousin."

He was visibly shaking. "No one should see this thing twice."

"I don't want to see it ever again," I said. "That's why I need you and Takelot to work your memories. I want to know everything you remember about that other time."

"I'll tell him. But there isn't much to add to what we told you before."

"There may be something you don't even realize you remember."

I found Smendes, gazing down at the figure. "Did you know him well?"

"He was Army-mad like so many youngsters. He'd watch the marches, practice the sword-drills, but Pharaoh had seen enough sons die in battle or from the illnesses that follow armies to permit him to join when he grew to maturity."

"Where do you think he came from tonight?"

"I cannot tell. He and his brothers were down in Punt. Do you know the country?"

"I've never been. An important trading partner with Egypt, right?"

"Most of our exotic goods from through there. Ivory. Spices. Cedar and sandalwood. If it's expensive, it comes from Punt."

A hint of jealousy in his tone, perhaps? Egyptian soldiers were paid no better than any other breed. Smendes might live in the luxury of the palace but he didn't own the place. I wondered if he was trying to support a palace lifestyle on a general's pay.

He had a motive, of course. Everyone spoke of him as Ramesses' successor even while at least several of Ramesses' sons had still lived. Would Pharaoh really pass over his own blood-line in favor of Smendes? Even a slight uncertainty could lead a doubtful heir to try other, magical methods to ensure a glorious future.

"But they aren't our partner," he added. "We own them, mostly." No Egyptian could ever admit otherwise. I've even heard some say Greece is nothing more than a vassal to Egyptian hegemony.

"Powerful magic..." I murmured when as the big guards came to lift up the poor boy.

"Gently!" We said it together.

Smendes sighed. "I hate all magic. It's a cheat, like poison or treachery. Kill a man if you must, standing up, sword to sword, skill against skill. No shadows, no secrecy." He spat.

"Some say this is a curse." I wasn't about to tell him who. If he didn't care for magic, what would he say to a bonafide ghost?

"Better to have stabbed Ramesses to the heart than attack him through his sons. I love that old man more than I ever did my own father. If you find out who has placed this curse on his house, tell me first of all. I alone shall take vengeance for it."

Once again, I bowed. Ramesses had chosen well, though his Smendes' fine words did not entirely convince me of his innocence. Anyone may claim these things. I wanted proof.

* * *

Though my clothes were all but dry, I reeked of the slimy smell of river water. More than that, I wanted to wash away my feelings of failure. I should have been able to save that boy, for the face, even distorted by the extremity of fear, had been no older than Hebnetma's.

I fought off the sleepy bath-girls. Like all palaces, rumors spread as though whispered on the wind and usually carry most of the truth. The girls looked at me with pity more than with dread. Regardless, they left me alone.

Laying in the water, adrift with my thoughts, I tried to piece everything together. When I felt I knew what questions to ask, I shook myself like a dog, dressed in my own cleaned and pressed clothes. Then I went looking for the answers.

My first task was to wake up Meryt by whatever means necessary. I headed toward the women's hall, brushing past the door guards as they'd been the statues they resembled. "Hey now...."

"I want the Lady Aimut on His Majesty's business."

"I knew you weren't any assistant scorpion killer."

Lady Aimut appeared almost before her maid went to find her. She clutched a robe to her body, blinking at me with eyes already red from weeping. "The rumor is that they found Kemes. Is it true?"

"Yes. I'm sorry; was he your son?"

"I gave my lord only daughters. I used to grieve for that but now I know I was blessed by the Spiritual Mother Herself." She glanced over her shoulder. A quavering keening arose from the rear of the hall, a chorus of many mourning voices. "In a way, however, he was a son to all of us...as were the others."

When she understood what I wanted, she summoned several older sister-wives. They were as efficient as removing the effects of too much beer from a reluctant waker as Petta's girls when the paid hour was up. However, when the herbal infusions, cold tea and a feather down her throat had done all that they could, I scooped her up and dropped her bodily into a cold bath.

She screamed and came fighting, her eye makeup running and her wig floating beside her. I stopped her tirade with the words, "Pharaoh wants to see you."

Her eyes grew huge. "My children...."

"Come, my dear," Aimut said kindly. "Accept the loan of a few garments until yours can be dried."

Aimut and her sister-wives much have filled Meryt in on the horrors of the night for she walked silently beside me. She glanced at me from time to time as if to read my face. I didn't give much away. "Eno," she whispered at last. "Will you help me?"

"I have too many clients already, including your son."

We were stopped outside Pharaoh's entryway. These guards weren't chosen for looks.

"Where are my children?" Meryt asked as we waited.

"I haven't seen Hebnetma since dinner."

"And Naunet?" she asked a long time later.

"Her father is, no doubt, taking thought for her."

Meryt put her hands over her face, staggered a few steps and went to stand facing the corner. When Smendes came out, he glanced at her curiously, but said nothing to her.

He'd also taken the time to change. He wore the striped kilt of a high-ranking officer. The sharp edges of his wig suited his grim features. About his neck he wore the Golden Fly on a heavy gold chain. An unidealized model of a common fly, this is the Egyptian's greatest award for valor. Given perhaps no more than twice in a generation, it is the ultimate honor except for the *pshent* itself, the Double Crown representing a united Egypt.

"He will see you now."

I had to take Meryt by the elbow to guide her in. She shook in my grasp like a sail under weak wind. She gasped when the heavy double doors, twice as tall as I am, shut behind us.

Ramesses sat in a highly decorated throne, up three broad steps. The very first light of dawn slipped in through remote windows, reflecting off brass plates to shine down into the hall. It found his broad beaded collar, the flail and the crook he held in his hands, and the misery of his face beneath the lapis-blue of the ceremonial crown, the *khepresh*. The bulbous front was decorated with a rising cobra in gold and precious stones.

Two priests waited either side of him, dressed in the full leopard-skin panoply of their office. A scribe, seated on a leather cushion, dipped a sharpened quill into a pot of ink, preparing to take down every word. The effect couldn't have been more impressive if they'd brought in the Royal Army's Marching Band.

Meryt moaned aloud. "I knew this day must come. I have dreaded its approach with every nightfall, thinking that surely tomorrow all would be revealed." Her eyes were red-rimmed and her voice rasped from vomiting. She fell to her hands and knees, her forehead on the floor. "Forgive me, greatest and most terrible of all the kings of the earth."

"Make to us your fullest confession." His voice sounded as though it came strained through the vast depths of time. This was not the kindly old gentlemen I'd met in the back garden nor the grieving father. This was God-on-Earth, the living manifestation of Ra, the Horus of Gold.

Meryt raised up on her knees, hands lifted prayerfully before her. Despite her fear, I felt somehow that she was almost enjoying the situation. Not everyone got to figure prominently in a legend come to life.

"I am Meryt-Amun, currently resident of the Great Temple at Thebes. Before that, I was married to Paser, the corn-factor here at Tanis. My father was a farmer in the village of Pasmenet by the Fourth Cataract."

Ramesses sat up a little straighter. Something in her words had caught his interest. From behind his throne stepped Aimut, attired as befitted a great lady, attended by two lesser women. She had been introduced to me as a senior wife. Standing there, gazing down at Meryt, she could have been a queen.

Meryt went on. "There, the Son of Heaven chanced to glimpse my sister, Senisonbe, as she worked her loom in the evening on the roof of our house."

"We remember Senisonbe the Golden."

"She came to the palace at my lord's command, not this one, the Great House in the center of the city. I married and came to live here in Tanis as well. There was an old watchman who would let her leave the palace alone and she would often come to visit me. We grew heavy with the fruit of our lords at the same time. It's often so with sisters."

"I remember her as well," Aimut said softly, and dropped her hand on the arm of the throne. Ramesses put down his flail and covered her hand with his own.

"I was filled with joy, but Senisonbe with sorrow. She felt trapped by the protocols of the court. She had been used to weaving and cooking, to visiting the marketplace, to meeting freely with her friends. All were forbidden her. Oh, they made light of her dislike of the idle life of a secondary wife to Pharaoh and she tried to make herself into a suitable member of the household. But she was bored and lonely. She would talk to me of the days at home, until the daylight faded and she would have to return."

Meryt paused, as though uncertain of what to say next. So far she'd been carried by the current of her memories of a beloved sister but now, as she came to the crux of the matter, every word could be used against her.

Pharaoh bade her to go on. She murmured something to her hands. Even I, close behind her, could not hear her. "Say it again," I prompted, wanting to know if my interpretation had been correct.

She glanced at me over her shoulder. Something of her pride and defiance returned. "When my time came upon me, she sought permission to stay with me. It was denied, she being near her own hour of strife. But when she heard I was in trouble, she slipped out anyway. My first son had been born easily. This one took hours and was born dead."

"A son?" Ramesses asked.

"Yes, he was perfect. But he was dead." She drew a heavy breath. "Even before my sorrow could ripen, Senisonbe's pains came upon her. I, my maid, my midwife did all we knew for her. But a darkness lay over my husband's house that day. Not all our prayers to Bes, to Bastet, to Sekhmet the All-Powerful to spare her life availed. Our prayers only ensured that the child, a girl-child, came into this world in the fullness of health and beauty."

Meryt raised her right hand high. "As Senisonbe lay dying, the color fading from her cheeks, she grasped this hand of mine and begged me with tears to take Naunet for my own. Above all things, she wished for her child to escape the misery her mother had known, living in the palace. She put her child into my arms and ordered the midwife to bring my dead son to her. She died cradling his cold body. So they were found by the Household Guards who came in search of her. So were they buried."

She looked fully into the face of Pharaoh. "I knew it was wrong; I expect no mercy and desire none. I stole a child of the God."

Turning again to me, she reached out to touch the sword hanging by my thigh. "Take this and slice me to pieces. Execute the full severity of the law upon me. But know, oh, Ramesses, that I would do the same again."

Her voice choked and died. She put a trembling hand to her cheek, looking in wonder at the tears on her fingertips. Then she covered her face and wept.

Aimut came slowly down the steps of the throne, her attendants beside her. She gazed down at Meryt for a long moment, then touched her fleetingly on the head. Meryt looked up. Then Aimut knelt beside her. "I beg for mercy for this woman. The wrong she did was for love's sake. I beg for mercy."

"None who ask for mercy before this throne shall be denied it. But the girl known as Naunet must be informed of her true status and take up her proper place in the hierarchy of the kingdom. Only thus will harmony return to this land."

Without turning his head, he pointed at the scribe. "Let the verdict of Pharaoh be known to all. Naunet is the true fifteenth daughter of Ramesses, and of his wife Senisonbe, the Golden Tear in the Treasure House of Pharaoh."

After the women left, Ramesses dismissed his priests and his scribe, handing them his regalia. He lifted the crown from his head. "I've always liked this one the best," he said with a smile at me. "It's not as heavy as the Double Crown."

"I've always thought crowns must be uncommonly uncomfortable. I don't understand why so many men hanker after them so."

"There are, sometimes, compensations. I will be delighted to meet Senisonbe's daughter. I wonder if she is as beautiful as her mother. I remember her so very well."

"Did you really just see her in passing?"

"I was forty. I thought life could hold no more for me. I had wives, sons, a mighty kingdom." He sat down on the bottom step and waved me to a similar seat. "I was returning from a drive when I got lost. You wouldn't think a man could get lost so long as he stayed close to the river but I did. I came upon this tiny village, maybe twelve houses, just at sunset. I saw...."

He smiled at the memory. "I saw a golden flame on the roof of a house. I was just about to shout 'fire' when I saw that it was a maiden, her sunlit hair growing in golden twists like fine wire. I stopped so short my horses stumbled. She looked over the edge and laughed at me."

His eyes clouded over as he gazed into the past. "No one ever laughed at me at home. I had many wives, every one of them busy with children, or complaints, or placidly awaiting my pleasure. Only this girl laughed. So I stayed in that village for a week; I believe I was given up for lost in the desert. I married her before I left, instructing her to follow after me when she'd collected her household goods."

"What happened?"

"I met her at the gates, with many chariots, a parade guard, my wives and children to strew her path with flowers, and a suite of slaves to tend her every whim. I myself placed a diadem on her head and shod her feet with golden sandals. But the light went out of her eyes when she saw who I really was. She'd thought she had married a simple soldier. There was no joy in her for Pharaoh."

Ramesses stood up, his knees creaking audibly. "How long should I give them, do you think?"

"I'm sure Lady Aimut will send for you when Naunet is prepared. You might...leave off the gold."

CHAPTER THIRTEEN

I seemed destined to have more or less miserable boat trips during this case. The crew and passengers were sharply aware of the macabre cargo they carried. Meryt's weeping at parting from her beloved child was audible in every part of the ship. Hebnetma, traveling to make his report to his uncle, drooped damply because, in addition to his confusion over his changed family, he proved to be violently sea-sick, even on a river. I'd been spared knowing that about him previously, though it did explain why he was so ravenous after the trip. Nothing stayed down.

Compounding the general air of gloom was the behavior of the locals as we passed. Whatever side wind had informed the palace inmates of young Kemas' fate had blown outside its walls as well. Word had spread as anonymously and as easily as chaff that a scion of the Royal House had passed on into death's domain.

All the way from Tanis to Thebes, the banks on both sides were thronged with humanity. Crones whose ages seemed to rival the Pyramids knelt on the sand, wailing with grief. Men wept openly, palms to their eyes as they swayed to and fro. Younger women poured handfuls of dirt onto their heads, abasing their beauty now that Kemas was not there to see it. Every breath was accompanied by the sounds of mourning.

I was never more happy to see a city than to see Thebes, glorious in the sunrise.

Messengers had been set ahead, bearing news of our arrival to the High Priest. I was eager for a talk with him. Ramesses had seemed certain that his father's revered ghost would no longer haunt Naunet, now that she was openly acknowledged as a daughter. The old king had a deeply ingrained sense of family and we learned that his appearances had coincided with the girl's maturity. Apparently, he'd been satisfied with her situation until it had been arranged for her to marry a mere nobody, outraging the old king's sense of the fitness of things.

Ramesses had suggested that Naunet make sacrifices and leave gifts at her grandfather's tomb. If only to persuade him to stay put, she'd agreed. Ramesses was going to make her a handsome allowance, the same as his other daughters. He seemed pleased with her, her charm, her ready laugh, her way of making an instant confidante of everyone. Though shy of him at first, she soon offered him an unguent for his sore knee 'to be rubbed in thoroughly three times a day! Never mind if it smells a bit, will you?"

"No, indeed. Evil smells drive out evil spirits."

"So they say. But, personally, I believe that it's the stinging nettles that does the most good."

He spent perhaps an hour in her company, listening to her chatter and exclaim over the pretty dresses and jewelry Aimut had unearthed. They'd all belonged to her mother. She'd put on a pair of earrings and flirted a feather fan as she peered at herself in a polished bronze mirror. Then she put the fan down and drew her hand away slowly.

"You are my father?"

"I am. I have attested it before the Gods."

"This Lady Senisonbe was my mother?"

"You have a great look of her at times."

"I don't wish to dispute with you," she said, meeting his eyes shyly. "I have, however, only one mother. I -- I could not be happy if we were parted forever."

"You have nothing to fear," he answered. "You must part for a short time, for Meryt-Amun owes a duty to her brother-in-law to return and show him that all is well with his family. But she will not be forbidden to enter here or to see you whenever you wish it."

"I only wish Thebes were not so far off."

He laughed and rose from his chair. Kissing her forehead, he said, "I would do much for you, grant every whim. I cannot, however, fold the Nile to bring that city closer."

I would have followed him from the room but Naunet motioned frantically to me. "I don't understand. I went to bed a corn-factor's daughter and wake up a princess. Whatever next? Shall I wake up in a cloud and walk upon the air as your gods do in the Great Green?"

"I hope not. At any rate, at least your ghost won't trouble you any further."

"He must have been very remarkable to come back all the way from the Other Side of the River just for me. My own grandfather and no one knew it. I suppose the real man does look different than the statues they've made of him. Older, for one thing."

I didn't want to discuss statues of any kind. "He wanted you to be acknowledged by everyone as a rightful member of the royal family."

"So Lord Ramesses said. I'm only surprised Grandfather didn't tell me about it himself, though perhaps he was wise. Who would have believed me? They just would have thought me insane and put lamb's fat and ashes on my head."

"What?"

"It's a famous remedy for insanity." Naunet touched the linen robes on the bed, each woven of cloth so fine that it was all-but transparent. "It feels very strange to find I was of royal blood all along. I never guessed. I always thought princesses were different than everyone else, touched by heaven's grace or something."

"Your mother explained everything...that is, Lady Meryt did."

"She kept breaking down and crying. Lady Aimut told me most of it." Her soft brown eyes were troubled. "It's a sad story, that Senisonbe would rather die than live here, with her lord, with all these beautiful things."

"Some people cannot be caged, unless they forge the bars for themselves. She probably would have been happy enough if her husband had been an ordinary man who could let her live as a free woman."

"I never want to be married to an ordinary man."

Before, that would have been her cue to remind me that I was supposed to be the one for her. Or so all the oracles had claimed. This time, however, she'd begun to turn the bracelet upon her wrist, a dreaming smile on her lips. If someone had supplanted me in her plans, that was all to the good, but I still would have liked to know who.

Come to think of it now, that bracelet had looked very much like the one Smendes had bestowed upon Meryt as a welcome gift. I couldn't recall if Naunet had been wearing the anklets. I was willing to bet, though, that she'd been wearing them when she bid him a shy farewell on the palace pier. She'd certainly been wearing enough of her other new finery and looking magnificent in all of it.

The ship drew up, in a moment reminiscent of our arrival at the riverside palace at Tanis, beside a long dock running to the river from the Great Temple. The temple was larger by far than the Pharaoh's summer palace. Every white-faced limestone block bore a deeply inscribed set of hieroglyphs, brilliantly and freshly painted with strong pigments, including the prized lapis blue and malachite green, ground from the stones themselves. It must have cost an absolute fortune.

The High Priest, Wadjmose, looked to have been a fine, strong man once, nearly as tall as I am. It is hard to judge the age of a man who has lived in prayer, in darkened temples, bound by rituals half as old as time. However old he might be, he looked every hour of it. He had triple pouches beneath his reddened eyes and long grooves worn in each cross-hatched cheek. His hands trembled as he lifted them to bless his nephew and sister-in-law's return.

"Are you well, Uncle?" Hebnetma asked gravely.

"Yes, my boy, perfectly well." When he turned his dark eyes toward the ship, bearing the body of Kemes in a hastily built coffin, he clasped his hands together and raised them shaking to his forehead as if he'd club his own brains out. "This is a terrible, terrible thing," he said in a choked voice.

He turned to Smendes. "How is our Lord bearing up under these...fresh horrors?"

"He is resolute in his faith in the Gods," the general said. Though he'd put aside his awards and badges of office, he wore his uniform of striped linen and a sharply creased headwrap. A strap ran over his chest, holding a battered scabbard.

"Yes, we must remember the Gods," Wadjmose said. "I pray, you know, without ceasing, begging them to lift this terrible curse from our beloved king. All our brothers pray for it. We neglect almost every other office."

He looked behind him as if in surprise at the mourning priests and servants who came out from the temple to honor the dead. Like their country friends and relations, they were making the fullness of their grief known. Their frenzied misery stood in stark contrast to the serene, otherworldly calm on the faces of the long run of stone sphinx, the bodies of cats and the heads of rams, that lined the road from the temple. They were so realistic that I almost expected to see them rise, shake off the humans who dared weep over their backs, and stalk off with a sheeplike 'humph!'

"We are all trying very hard indeed to awaken the Gods' compassion upon our poor Egypt. But come, you must be refreshed after your journey."

General Smendes forestalled the High Priest's attempt to escort us into the temple. "I have strict instructions that there is to be no delay in laying young Kemes in his burial chamber with his brothers. If you will be so good as to give the orders that will expedite my task...."

"Certainly, General. My assistant, Harsiese, will help you in any way possible." He waved over a priest from the front row of mourners and Smendes instantly began rattling off what he needed and how he wanted everything organized. I could tell the young priest was already far behind and losing ground by the moment. When he asked for something to be repeated, Smendes took him by the shoulder and marched him over to the boat.

The High Priest began working his fingers together as if trying to milk them. His eyes squeezed shut as he mumbled something. My shadow chanced to fall across him as the sun grew higher. He spun around sharply, gasping.

"Who are you? What do you want?" he demanded in a pettish, high-pitched tone as if he hadn't noticed me standing just a few feet away. It piqued my interest as people don't usually overlook me.

"I'm Eno the Thracian. Ready-to-hire adventurer, skilled in both defense and attack, arranger of discreet negotiations, and contender with madmen, monsters and ladies in distress. Confidentiality guaranteed, which means I won't talk even if everyone else can't shut up."

"Eno? Yes, I did send for you. Now that I see you, I understand your reputation. You were described to me as more than a man, indeed."

"Reputation lies. I am only a man." In this land of strange gods, before one who'd dedicated his life to them, I wasn't about to make any claims of divine parenthood. They might believe me and, if they didn't, Naunet's recipe for curing insanity sounded absolutely disgusting. "What can I do for you?"

"Much, perhaps. I had begun to despair, that all is for naught. Perhaps you have been sent by the Mighty Ra to succor our poor people. I don't know any more. The signs are confused." He squinted up at the sun, a burning blur in the blue. "I have not time to speak of these matters now. I must offer the service for this hour."

Turning to go, he stumbled. Hebnetma stepped forward swiftly to support him. "You are ill, Uncle."

The High Priest patted him reassuringly on the upper arm. "Nay, my boy, I am merely tired. I promise I shall rest after we lay this poor soul in this tomb. If I may make use of you to aid Brother

Thut and Brother Harsiese with the arrangements? Thut is coordinating the ceremony with the Anubians. Perhaps he would be grateful for a little help. They are not a cooperative cult, I'm afraid."

"Of course. Whatever I can do to help."

Wadjmose smiled at him and, rather vaguely, at me. He seemed a kindly sort, a little wobbly on his legs, prone no doubt to wind and forgetfulness in small matters. He'd go on saying his prayers by rote until he was a hundred and ten and probably drop dead halfway through a service. Several other priests hurried to him as he headed into the temple grounds. His staff of office, headed by a golden cheetah with lapis eyes and spots, was more a prop than a symbol at this point.

Hebnetma said, "He is failing so quickly. Even in these few months that we've been gone, I can see the change."

"What do his doctors say?"

"That he must spare himself. That he must rest and let others carry some of his duties and burdens. He promises to do so but there is always a reason he does not."

"You're home again. You'll be able to help him."

"Will you, Eno? Whatever he wants you to do, take on the task. Anything to relieve him of some of this terrible weight. It was bad enough when he had only the temples of Egypt to tend. Now he has half the country upon his shoulders. And now, to add to it all, this business about Naunet."

He dug the toe of his sandal into the white gravel walk and looked miserable and embarrassed as only a young man can. On his face, the emotions were amplified until he looked like the sum of all unhappy youth throughout time. I wanted to weep myself, just from looking at him.

"I don't know how I'll explain about Naunet. He's always been so fond of her."

"Surely that won't change."

"He's always talking about how much we resemble our father...I mean, my father."

"People see what they think is there. I'm sure he won't change his attitude toward her; why should he?"

"Maybe. I'm sure he'll feel differently about my mother, though." He sighed. "I just don't understand how she could act so foolishly. She must have known it would all come out some day."

"Try to think of it from her point of view."

"I can't. Women don't think about things the way we men do. They don't think things through." He sighed again, more heavily yet. "Well, I'd better go see what help I can be."

I was not left at a loose end for long. Smendes came over to me and asked if I were ready to go. "Go where?"

"The tomb. I want to go ahead of the funeral procession to make sure all's well out there. I've just been told there were rock-slides in the Valley two or three weeks ago and no one has been out there to make sure the entrance to the tomb has been cleared. They sent a work-party out last week but who knows if they've finished yet."

It seemed odd to me that Smendes would go himself instead of sending a couple of flunkies. But when we crossed the river, I understood.

Waiting for us on the far side were two chariots, the latest style with six-spoke wheels and curved wicker-worked bodies with the new slashes to lighten the load and increase the speed. Fine horses were already hitched to the single bar. The brown ones shook their heads, setting the small bells in their braided manes jingling, while the white pair pawed at the ground. The plumes on their heads moved in the hot breeze from the desert beyond.

"Can you drive?" Smendes asked.

"I've driven Scythian war-chariots but nothing quite this slick," I said.

"You want to watch the turns. Stand with a foot on each side to flatten out, or your wheel will rise up and a spill at top speed isn't healthy." He stepped into the chariot drawn by the white horses and shook his head when the stand-by driver tried to join him in the basket. "We won't be long," he said.

I took up my reigns. "'Course there's no real future for me in chariot racing; I'm too heavy. Still...worth a try."

It wasn't easy to get the hang of it. The Egyptian terrain is very well suited for racing on two wheels in a flimsy crate. Hit any rock bigger than a walnut and the only thing keeping you in the chariot is your grip on the leather straps. But don't pull too hard or you'll turn your horses' heads and go into a skid.

Meanwhile, tiny rocks thrown up by your wheels go popping around your head like bees, stinging your cheeks and arms. The bastard you're racing, without quite knowing why you are except he got such a good start you can't help but try to catch up, is throwing up a choking dust. Every time you try to get clear of the cloud, he swerves at the last instant so that you can't get past without running into him, meanwhile throwing up even more dust.

Of course, it was futile. I must have outweighed Smendes by fifty pounds, even with his bit of a belly. No way the leggy, light-bodied horses used in Egypt could drag me and a chariot past him. I wondered how a couple of cart-horses would fare and decided they, like me, would be better off pulling a plow. In Egypt, though, they use oxen for that. Horses are the breath of the Gods made flesh and are saved for only the nobility and the army.

Before us appeared a long canyon, widening out like arms to greet us. The heat seemed to collect there, breathing out upon us like the opening in a kiln. It even smelled like hot clay taken directly from the oven. The only color was the sky, and even that had paled with the sun at zenith to the pale blue of the water sapphires I'd fished from mountain streams when I was a boy. I wished I had about ten drops from one of those streams now.

Smendes pulled up with a sweeping flourish before a small work-party of troops who cheered when they saw him. I, close on his heels, received only a few doubtful glances. Obviously I was not fated to be popular.

They'd been clearing a rock fall away from a cliff base. Every yard of the cliff seemed identical to every other pile of rock in this valley. There wasn't a bit of difference between one boulder and the next, one grain of sand and all the others. This was the Gate to the Valley of the Kings, the burial place of Egyptian royalty, and a more dreary final resting place could hardly be imagined.

Grave robbers and the law had been outsmarting each other over the grave goods from here ever since the first tomb was opened. Even now, someone could be watching from the top of these cliffs, watching every move we made, marking what we did. It would explain the creepy feeling I'd gotten the second the chariot had stopped and I'd stepped off.

The location of the sacred royal burial chambers was supposed to be a dead secret. In truth, everyone knew about it. No one spoke about it exactly because everyone already knew. Who would you tell?

The General called the scarred veteran sergeant by name, agreed with him that new recruits were essentially useless, pinched one young lad's ear, cracked a joke with another and left them, dusty and tired as they were, feeling like they'd just won a battle.

"We must leave our swords with the sergeant," Smendes said to me, as he began to unbuckle his chest-strap.

"Oh?"

"Sacred ground. No weapon that has ever been used in anger may be permitted beyond the lintels of the door."

I hooked a thumb toward the cliff wall. "But they're buried with all sorts of things for the afterlife, even arrows and knives?"

"They are. Ceremonial weapons only. They have no need of weapons of war in a land where all is peace and plenty."

"True." It seemed reasonable so I handed my sword to the sergeant. His eyes widened as he took the weight of it in his hand. "It's kind of special," I said. "Don't let the kids play with it."

In the instant I'd looked away, Smendes had vanished. The soldiers snickered behind their hands. I walked closer to the cliff wall and saw a shadow, no bigger than my thumb beside one of the slabs of rock. I twisted my neck to the side, letting one eye go out of focus, and saw an entrance appear as if manifesting itself from the living rock. I took a mere half-step back and it was gone again. You could walk by this spot every day of your life and never know it was there. The cave entrance was covered by the slab as though each had been carved to match. Maybe they had been.

I knew I was delaying on purpose. I don't like caves or any small, dark place. Nothing good ever happens in one and they tend to be occupied by things that, one way or another, want to kill me. A tomb is too much like a cave with the added disquiet of dead people.

I slipped in behind the stone, brushing my shoulders against the rough sides of the entry. Once a cave formed by nature, it was now improved by man to be wide, sloping, and perfectly smooth after the first twenty feet or so. I sniffed, relieved that there seemed to be plenty of fresh air.

I tried not to think about the tons of rock above my head. I tried not to think about that tiny entrance getting buried under another slide, too great for the troops outside to clear. I tried not to think about these things and failed.

Torches burned on the walls, flickering restlessly in the draft from the entrance. Rooms opened up beyond the central chamber. Here pillars painted with lotus and papyrus supported a ceiling high enough for me to stand up-right. The other chambers were lower and narrower. They seemed filled with some kind of rubble, probably left over from the building of the main chamber.

There, the sons of Pharaoh stood, forever frozen in the form they'd taken when they'd died. Some were composed, resolute despite their fear. Some had turned to run and died anyway. Others had fallen to their knees. But there were nowhere near as many of them as I had expected. Where were the others?

"General?"

"Over here."

I found him beside a chamber on the far side of the tomb. He held a torch low and was looking at the rubble and pebbles piled within. "These were the first. Sherat, Paramesse, Tenermentu, and more. All of the sons of Pharaoh's first three wives."

"How long ago was that?"

"Eight times have the waters of the Nile overflowed their banks since Sherat was the first to be struck down."

"But the stones...why are they all broken? Some ritual?"

"At first, they seem to be strong rock, just as any other statue carved by men. After only a few months, they began to crumble. Now you can almost see time eating away at them as though one day encompasses many months."

The evidence lay tumbled on the ground. I glanced at the others, still with the outward form of men. "Is there any legend in your lands of a monster than can do this sort of thing? Or any god?"

I wondered how he'd take the insult to one of his deities. Smendes, though, wasn't the kind of man to take offense at a question asked only for clarification. "Not that I've ever heard of. The High Priest says the same and he would surely know for he has searched through all the sacred writings. I have heard, though, of a creature from your land that can turn men to stone."

"Who's that?" I thought for a moment. "Oh, you must mean gorgons."

"A virgin priestess who broke her holy vows to her virgin goddess and lay with a man," Smendes said solemnly. "Her goddess punished her by turning her into a creature of such surpassing hideousness that all who looked upon her turned to stone."

"Yeah, I know that old story. Poisonous green adders for hair and all that. But it's not true."

"Not true? You do have such monsters in your lands, such as have been utterly banished by Egyptian civilization."

I ignored the dig. "Oh, we have monsters. Big ones. Ugly ones. Ones that'll bite you in half and others that will just nibble you to death. But gorgons couldn't do this kind of damage to a fully-grown man, not even if you got a hundred of 'em together at the same time."

"I don't understand."

"Gorgons are little dragons," I said, holding my hands about a foot apart. "They live in shallow caves up in the mountains, Delos and Crete, places like that. They hardly ever come out except just at dawn. That whole 'turning to stone' thing is an exaggeration. They fascinate small prey by holding them with their eyes and then biting them quickly with mildly poisoned fangs. If they miss, the prey runs off and the gorgon goes hungry. They're kind of cute, though I don't recommend them as a family pet."

"Maybe an especially big one?"

"They don't get big. I saw one in a traveling circus once that was maybe as long as my arm and it was billed as the largest in the world."

"I see. Well, you've been very helpful."

"Sorry. No," I said, "this smells like magic to me and has right along. Powerful magic, like from a mad wizard or a sorcerer who's been messing around with the Dark Powers. What we've got to do is...."

I'm never sure what it is that makes me turn around a mere instant before someone tries to brain me with a rock. Certainly it would be more sensible to turn around two or three minutes beforehand so I could say, "What are you going to do with that rock?" instead of throwing myself violently aside just before impact.

CHAPTER FOURTEEN

The first rock, and I hoped it was an honest rock and not a former body part, came directly at my head. I dodged, hitting the wall hard. There was hardly enough room to move at this end of the burial chamber so I shuffled back as fast as I could toward the largest room. Smendes stooped for another piece of stone.

"Have you lost your mind?" I demanded.

"I can't let you live with what you know." He grunted as he threw the stone. His aim was pretty good. It bounced off my shoulder. Instinctively, I grabbed for my sword but it, of course, was outside. Not that it would have been much good against a thrown rock.

In another instant, I was out of sight behind the first pillar. Taking him for my example, I also stooped for a rock, this one more or less round. Thankfully, it looked too big for a skull.

I bowled it away, sending it crunching along the hard-packed floor, hoping it would sound like running feet to Smendes. He came quickly around the pillar. I jumped him, getting in a few solid punches into the triangle of his mid-section. He connected with my jaw which didn't rock me much. His next shot was over my heart which would have killed me if he'd had a knife.

I gave him a crisp, short uppercut that threw his head back as though he'd run his chariot into the cliff-wall of the Valley. I followed it with a belt over the ears that must have set his head to ringing but he rattled in again and got a fist to my nose. First blood to him.

He lunged at me, taking me down in a forward rush. Though I was no champion, I'd studied enough wrestling to know how to recover from a fall like that. I clasped my hands together for a rabbit-punch on the back of his neck but changed to trying to throw him off instead. I didn't want to kill him, after all. I wished he felt the same way about me.

We struggled silently. He didn't seem to want to yell for his friends and I had nothing much to say. Questions could wait until I had won. For a minute or two, neither of us had the advantage. When he tried to bite me, though, I'd had enough.

I wove my arm through both of his, pulling them back into chicken-wings. I threw a leg over his top-side knee, pinning him. With my other hand, I dragged his head back to a strained hold. 'If you try that again, I'll break your neck," I said.

He struggled with everything he had for a few seconds, twisting and surging like a half-broken horse. Red in the face, he took a few breaths and tried again. I tightened the hold until I knew he was just this side of agony.

"Get off!" He said a couple of other things as well, though his speech was unclear through having his face pushed into tomb-dust.

"Is calling me 'fat lummox' really the tone you want to take right now?"

"You can't kill me," he said. "The guards would never let you get past."

"I don't want to kill you," I protested. "Unless you're the one turning all these poor sods to stone."

"Of course it's not me!"

"It's hard to tell with sorcerers, warlocks, and the like. They can look normal, just like anybody, when they want to. True, they do tend to run to the black leather, studs, and curly-toed slippers look. Doesn't mean they have to stick to that. There's no rule about it or anything."

"Look, I'm not a sorcerer."

"Prove it." We both waited. "You see, it's impossible. The Greeks figured that out years ago; you can't prove what isn't true."

"Let me up."

"Why? You're just going to grab another rock."

"No, I won't. No rocks, no sticks, no swords, not even a suspicious chariot race." It worried me that he'd given the possible methods of my demise so much thought. "I swear it by Amun-Ra."

Against my better judgment, I let him up. That was the ultimate oath now in Egypt. They used to be two gods but someone combined them a dozen years or so ago.

He tried to brush off his uniform, a hopeless task. The meticulously groomed general resembled a small boy after a day playing 'war'. I probably looked about as bad. I squeezed my nose with due tenderness. It wasn't broken, but no one's appearance is improved by having a beetroot for a nose.

"So?" I asked. "Why the sudden urge to smash my head in with a rock? Was it something I said?"

"Something you will say."

I kept a wary eye on him. Nothing had happened in the last five minutes to make him stop wanting to kill me. Quite the reverse as I'd just wrestled him into capitulating which probably wounded his Egyptian pride, the like of which few nations can boast.

"You spent several nights alone with my...with Naunet. You debauched her, defiled her...."

"Wait just a second," I said, holding up my hand. "No, I didn't. Nothing happened. We were too busy running away from monsters, visiting gods, and tending to a small baby boy to get up to anything. You just ask her some time. Not that I would have anyway."

"You don't find her the most desirable of women?" He took an angry step forward.

"No. I mean, she's charming, don't get me wrong. A nice girl if you like 'em that way. But she's a little young and sprightly for my taste. I like mature, serious women." At least I did when said young girl's lover wants to scramble my brains with the nearest rock.

His hot brown eyes turned as miserable as a lonely dog's. "And too young for me as well."

"Oh, I don't know. She could probably use a sturdy man to keep a hand on the reigns. Lightly, you know. Guiding her more than controlling her."

"But you don't deny you took her away with you," Smendes demanded. I knew he was in love but I was getting dizzy from the mood-swings.

"That was her mother's doing."

"Indeed?" he scoffed.

"Meryt was so desperate to save her from the terrible fate of becoming a princess that she was willing to do anything, even tell her to follow a strange man into the hills, to keep her from suffering like Senisonbe. I wonder if the oracles said anything about me at all. Or was that more of Meryt's scheming."

"Most women scheme to place a daughter among Pharaoh's wives, even if he has ceased to play ewes and ram."

"They're an unusual family. Hey, why is everyone making such a fuss over young

Hebnetma?" I asked, partly because I really wanted to know and partly because it seemed a good time to change the subject.

"Oh, everyone expects Wadjmose to name the boy as his successor as he has no children of his own now living."

"What happened to them? Not...?" I patted the shoulder of a stone man.

"No. Just ordinary things, sickness, one drowned, I think." He dusted his hands and I relaxed imperceptibly. "They've been grooming the nephew for the role for some years. It's why they sent him on that diplomatic mission. The High Priest is also ruling half the country and they felt he needed some foreign exposure."

"And now his sister is an acknowledged daughter of Pharaoh. Quite a change. Which couldn't be better for you. If you are named heir, you marry the girl and she further legitimizes your succession."

"I don't care about that. I will serve my country and my king no matter what."

I could tell he still had doubts about what happened in the hills of my own country. He'd probably have doubts right up until their wedding night. I didn't think I'd stick around for the ceremony.

"Look," I said. "All I want to do is find out what the High Priest wants me to do, do it, get paid, and go back to Kalithanos. I've got some unfinished business there."

We came out of the tomb not a minute too soon to suit me. Like I said, there always seems to be something in a tomb or a cave that wants me dead.

A slight haze of dust hung in the air far off past the entrance to the valley. Smendes shaded his eyes with his hand. "The procession. They'll be here soon."

He turned toward the troops and I tensed up again. If he gave the order to clout me on the head, bundle me on a chariot and lose me ten miles out, there wouldn't be much I could do about it. "Have you water enough to share?" he asked.

They'd been blatantly incurious about their general's unkempt state. The sergeant passed us each a terracotta water-bottle and we drank and rubbed the dust and dirt from our faces. Restored to a presentable, if not dapper, condition, we waited for the body to arrive.

I've attended too many funerals, even officiated at a few. Wherever the soul or spirit or 'ka' of a person is, their body is of no further interest to it. I'm not in favor of throwing bodies on garbage heaps or anything like that. Have a quick burial, a few quaffs of a suitable local beverage and a couple of words about how he was a good fellow who'd never stab you in the back or steal your spare cash and be done with it. I don't expect any more than that and I'll be lucky if I get it. They don't hold funerals for heroes who wind up on the inside of a monster in the course of employment.

An Egyptian funeral, however, is a sight everyone should see at least once. Like everything else, they have to do it differently than the rest of the world. For one thing, the whole ceremony is conducted by Anubis, not the real one. A priest of the cult, wearing an elaborate jackal mask, jet-black with touches of gold on the upstanding ears and eye-holes, incarnates the god.

It is a curious thing, standing there in the eye of the sun while the ceremony is going forward. You can see the human being's flaws, the dimpled chest where the muscle has gone, the thin legs, face probably pouring with sweat underneath the heavy mask. Yet, at the same moment, you feel strongly that is the god Himself come among you.

Usually there's a gap of several months between the death of a prince and the burial ceremony. They prepare the body with the famous mummification process, using a mixture of salts and other chemicals to preserve it for the tomb. With that habitation as a link, the spirit is free to pass through the doorway in either direction, toward the Eternal Paradise or to return to watch over descendants, as Ramsesses' father had done.

With poor Kemes, the death was too sudden. Though I doubted anyone here in Thebes knew him well, I saw genuine confusion and grief on the faces of the mourners. Even the priests seemed stunned. Tracks of tears furrowed the dust on deep brown cheeks.

The burial ceremony has many steps, each designed to ensure the safe passage of the spirit through the trials it must face before finding peace as well as to keep the link between human form and spiritual form. The Ceremony of the Opening of the Mouth, for instance, keeps the body as a conduit for sustenance. The beer and bread offering made by poor and rich alike, which feeds the spirit on the Other Side of the River, is vital to the health of the dead. The rich offer quite a few other things and, even for a hastily cobbled together funeral, they'd gotten together a chest full of necessities.

Finally, it was over. With a mostly-muffled groan, the bearers lifted him up and carried him within. There wasn't quite enough room behind the stone and I heard his transformed body grind against it as they passed. Everyone stood about aimlessly, until several of the priests started back. The female mourners followed them, chanting some ancient hymn in a half-forgotten dialect.

Smendes and I waited for the Anubian priest and the bearers to return. "I thought it went well," he said.

"As well as could be expected."

"Hasty business. He deserved better. They all did."

"So did his father. I can't imagine losing that many sons."

Smendes shook his head. "It's hard enough when it's soldiers," he said lowering his voice so the young troops would not hear. "That's the hardest part of being a commander. Watching the young ones die."

"Gods know it."

"Which army were you in?" he asked, just as if he hadn't tried to kill me.

"Croesus'. Good troops; lousy command."

"Ah, yes. When I joined up, what a mess. We hadn't won a major battle in thirty years, no matter what the scribes had chiseled onto monuments."

"Everybody exaggerates."

"Doesn't make it right," Smendes said. "They wanted to create a colonnade of stelae in my honor a couple of years ago. I put a stop to it. If my deeds can't live without a bunch of stone obelisks blaring them, then they weren't much to start with."

The bearers came out. The last one bowed and asked me to go in and meet with the priest. Smendes told me that he'd meet me back at the temple. I waited until he left, waving at him as the chariot flashed by.

If I hadn't liked the tomb the first time, I really didn't like it the second. It wasn't so much the new inhabitant, though he looked fine standing among his brothers. But I'd had a few too many close encounters with my own gods to risk meeting with foreign ones. It takes a lot out of a guy, talking to Supreme Beings.

"You wanted to see me?"

His voice echoed deeply. "You can help me."

"Of course."

"I'm stuck." He had his thumbs under the edge of the mask but seemed to lack the leverage to get it off.

I shook myself out of my self-imposed mystical fog and went to lift the mask off. It startled me with its weight and I noticed the red marks on the priest's shoulders before I noticed the priest.

"Your majesty?"

He wiped the sweat from his face. "I thought I'd never get free of it. Oh, don't look so surprised. I couldn't let them put Kemes here without attending myself."

"But officiating?"

"Why not? I'm a fully trained priest with an understanding of the rituals of most of the larger cults." He looked around the tomb and tears overflowed his eyes when he blinked. He wiped them away casually. "I hope they're all happy now. I'll see them again someday, I suppose. Sooner rather than later."

"We should step outside into the fresh air," I suggested.

"Yes." He stopped in the entrance. "Farewell, boys. It won't be long, I promise."

He staggered at least once as we walked out. I didn't know how to comfort him, for what comfort could there be for a man who had lost so much. I thought it best to change the subject.

"You have been instructed in many rituals?" I asked. I'd never heard of such a thing.

"Pharaohs have to be. Poor old Smendes is having a terrible time memorizing all of them. He got the Blessing of the Crocodile God mixed up with the Milking of the Great Cow. That did not go over well with the priests of either group, though Sekhmet's priestesses got quite the kick out of it all. Vicious lot of women, really."

I asked for a drink for the old man from the soldiers. As in his own palace, no one recognized him. One of them asked for his blessing on a late mother which he gave easily, then waved his hand over the others. "Your families are all well and happy in the service of the gods. Remember to make offerings with frequency."

I said, "I'll give you a lift back."

"Thank you. It's a long walk." When we reached the chariot, he ran his hand over the railing. "Nice looking thing. I haven't been in a chariot for maybe five years."

"Do you want to drive?"

"Oh, no. I've lost my taste for it. But once...once, no one could beat me."

I think he enjoyed it, despite his sorrows.

Dropping him off at the Temple to Anubis, he stood with the mask under his arm. "Tell no one you have seen me. I don't want anyone to know that I have left Tanis."

"Won't they know almost immediately?"

"I swore my body-servant to secrecy. He'll put off anyone who wants to see me. He's much less deaf than he pretends to be and gets a great deal of enjoyment from people trying to make him hear."

"I guess you've got to find your fun where you can."

"You have been kind to this old man, Eno. Will you do me another favor?"

"Yours is to command."

"So people say. Well, will you meet me here tonight, as close to midnight as you can?"

"What are you planning? And what is my part in it?"

"A journey into the desert. We may be gone some time." He flashed me a grin as happy as if no shadow had ever darkened his life. I did not pretend to understand him. How could a man bury so many of his children and still smile?

Yet, driving the team back to the temple compound, I thought of how he'd spoken to his dead sons, as though they could hear, could understand, and were only temporarily restricted from speech...and not necessarily even that. If their grandfather could come back as a ghost, why not the whole family? I wished wholeheartedly that I might discover who had cursed them. I wanted to see their spirits find justice, though I'd settle for vengeance.

People who don't believe in coincidences might consider the following.

"Let me see if I'm hearing you rightly, your eminence."

Wadjmose gave me the full attention of his mild, exhausted eyes for a moment, then resumed his restless pacing, hands behind his back. The ever-present scribe looked appreciative. Wadjmose had been rattling on at a good clip ever since I'd come in.

"Recap, by all means, my dear Eno."

"You want me to seek out whatever has destroyed the sons of Ramesses. To seek it and to stop it by whatever means necessary."

"Precisely. I have prayed ceaselessly, made daily, even hourly offerings, pleading for an answer to this horrible thing." That explained why he always looked asleep on his feet.

"You believe I'm your answer."

"I have been given signs from my Heavenly Master Himself. A light in the sky in the shape of a sword. The elevation of my dear niece after her meeting with you. The story of these two body-guards...present on two occasions when the ill befell a young prince."

Fjuti looked sheepish, standing in the corner of the priest's sanctuary. Takelot was apparently practicing to become a statue himself. He hardly breathed but could still look reproachfully at me. Apparently Smendes had insisted on hearing the same tale they'd told me over drinks and snacks back in Kalithanos, and then the general had told the priest everything. Small wonder Takelot wasn't feeling too happy with me. No one likes being brought to the attention of powerful people, especially ones who could stick you in the army and send you off to find some oasis so lost that it was contagious.

"These are just a few of the portents I have been given." He smiled distantly, keeper of the sacred mysteries to untutored barbarian.

"The Gods speak to me," he added, hitching up his leopard-skin. "Not always as clearly as I would prefer, of course. Their words are cryptic and only much study can unlock their meanings."

"Where do they suggest I look?"

"We will pray for a further answer. No doubt the Heavenly Father will guide our thoughts in the right direction."

"Maybe you could tell me where the other heroes you hired looked. Since they seem to have found what they were looking for." He'd already told me about the five others who had preceded me and who had died.

"We don't know that they were killed by this thing, whatever it may be. We have the bodies of only three. The other two may have simply run off, taking the advance money I paid them to start over somewhere else."

"No, your eminence," I said. "You see, I knew those men. They wouldn't do that. It's against the Hero's Code. Besides, the deaths are attested by half a dozen people a piece by what you've said. Definitely dead, if not turned to stone."

"They were none of them chosen, as you have been chosen. The Gods will protect you. I have seen it in the auguries. You cannot fail."

"More oracles," I said, but to myself.

"They do not lie, our Gods," he said fervently. "Any false readings are our failing to interpret their messages correctly. The fault is ours alone, our weak humanity betraying their perfection, our feeble inability to comprehend the glory of their ideas failing them again and again. If it weren't not for their infinite patience, they would destroy us all out of infinite frustration." He seated himself, sagging as if all his bones were softening.

"I will take on the job," I said, avoiding theology. "I'll leave immediately."

"Excellent." He bestowed a smile of me and a wave of blessing, a kindly gentleman grateful for cooperation. "I will give orders at once for your fee to be given to you. Bribe who you must, pay for information, be diligent and never count the cost. I would pour out the whole of the treasury to achieve this single aim. There must be a way to end this horror and I'm certain you will find it." He closed his eyes and swayed, not in any mystical way, but like a man falling irresistibly asleep.

The two cousins and I tip-toed out, followed by the scribe. "When he wakes up, tell him I've gone to follow up a lead. Better yet, have Hebnetma do it."

"I'll go with you to the bursar," Fjuti said. "He owes me and Takelot some back pay. I'll get him to give you what's been promised."

"All you need show him is this," the scribe said, handing me a piece of papyrus with what looked like a child's game sketched on it. "It's full authorization for your quest. May I wish you the very best of good fortune."

CHAPTER FIFTEEN

At last I was where I should have been all along, acting as official envoy for the High Priest of Amun. A sack of the needful hung from my belt and I had also a special seal that would act like a key to any building in Egypt, not excepting the Royal Houses. I could go anywhere, demand answers from anyone, and back up my requests with the full might of a religion that ordered both this life and the next.

The Hero's Code I'd mentioned made it very clear that 'the one who pays gives the orders' and that a good hero doesn't ask too many questions. He does the job, collects the fee, and goes home unscathed, please the gods.

Ordinarily, I'd play it just that way. I could even stretch this job out for a couple of weeks or decide the best place to look for a monster was the local tavern with the best-looking girls.

Not that I'd ever do a thing like that.

Yet, even so, I knew my loyalty did not lie with Wadjmose. I served firstly an old man's grief and the lives of his slaughtered sons. More than anything, I wanted to comprehend what had happened to the Sons of Ramesses and to stop it before it destroyed the last of them.

Furthermore, I'd begun to understand why Pan was so angry even though his children had been law-breakers and cannibals. Sooner or later, I was going to have to go back to Kalithanos and make amends as best I could for what I'd done. I only hoped it wouldn't prove too fatal.

I came on foot that night to the Temple of Anubis, a rough brown cloak, an old friend, thrown around my shoulders, a bag for necessities hung across my chest, and my sword at my hip. My eyes quickly adjusted to the dimness. Overhead, the Milky Way was as bright as a river of torches.

He was on the watch for me. It was the first time I'd ever seen him impatient. "You call this midnight? The moon passed over an age ago!" He cut my apology short. "Never mind, never mind. You're here now. I'd forgotten to tell you not to bring the chariot; clever of you not to."

He peered past me into the darkness. "You weren't followed?"

"If there was someone, I lost him."

"Was there?"

"I'm not certain. I thought I felt a presence so I dodged around some. It's second nature to me now."

Ramesses snorted. "As we travel, you must pass the time telling me your adventures."

"Where are we going, sire?"

"When the Medjai, the guards who report to no one save me, searched the riverbank where Kemes died, they found this." A pale piece of papyrus gleamed for an instant as it reflected the starlight. "He must have dropped it as he ran."

Ramesses held it out to me. I shook my head at it. "I can't read Egyptian even in broad daylight."

"Oh. Well, it is word from my last two remaining sons, Montu and Rudjek. They wait for word of safe passage before they venture once more onto our sacred soil. They drew lots for who would carry this message to me. Kemes lost. He was always very brave."

"Why in the name of Ganymede didn't they send a servant?"

"They all abandoned my sons, cowards and sons of cowards! The boys are alone, running low on food, but at a safe oasis above the First Cataract."

"That's a long way."

"I will not lose us in the desert, fear not."

"Well, it's your country."

"It is and a heavy burden I have found it," he said, sighing deeply. "At any rate, you and I are a rescue party."

Something large snorted in the darkness. I started and half-drew my sword. Ramesses motioned for me to put it away, saying, "Come and meet the rest of our party."

The dirty-beige creatures who waited beyond him were not, as I first thought, the product of a contemporary sculptor's diseased imagination, but living animals. Even in a country where they combine the most incompatible creatures, who but a madman would join together a swan's neck, a dog's face, the toes of a clam, and the humped back of a dragon?

"They're called what?"

"Camels. Long ago, when the wandering tribes of Israel came to this land, they brought these creatures along. We have never ceased to be grateful. They are the perfect pack animals for the desert."

"Do you ride on them? Or hitch them to a cart?"

"I don't do either. I lead them. These are ordinary camels, not the pure white ones bred for the royal service. Those are docile as kittens and even let me scratch them behind the ears."

"They have ears?"

Frankly, I'd rather walk a cat on a leash than try to persuade another camel that a stroll in my company was a congenial way to spend an evening.

Eventually, however, they decided of their own accord to walk more or less in the direction we wanted to go.

Once they began, they kept right on. I had not been in Egypt for quite a while and I had forgotten the narrowness of the arable land there. The Nile runs like a pulled thread through the center of the country. On either side of the great river, there is a strip of fertile land, black from the mud deposited when the river overflows as is does every year. And beyond the farm land...nothing.

Mile after mile of nothing. Tumbled blocks of stone, crumbled bits of rock, with no discernable difference in color or texture between that lump of rock there and this broken bit in my hand. Though some people might see a beauty in the austere landscape, to me it was just more rocks as far as my eyes could see. No variety, no charm, except perhaps to the eye of love.

I understood at last on the deepest level why the Egyptians called the lands beyond the Mediterranean Sea 'The Great Green'. It must seem like the only color that exists there just as beige now predominated in my mind. I began to hunger after greenery as much as for the touch of a sea-breeze or the cool tang of mountain air.

Ramesses must have loved the desert dearly for he perked up quite a bit as we went on. "I was never allowed to wander off, like other children. As soon as I could, I came out to this area and lived rough for a month. They never let me repeat the experiment; my mother found it too exhausting."

"She didn't go with you?" I couldn't imagine a pampered court lady out in the heat until I remembered that they were probably all village girls to start with.

"Oh, no. She simply worried and prayed and worried until I was home again. No one ever prays for you the way your mother does."

"And the High Priest of Amun," I muttered.

The sunrise brought a moment's excitement when all the stones and dust turned to the same shade as the reddened sun. Then it rose further, fading into a mere burning circle somewhere high in the sky. Even the shadows shrank away from the glare. Despite the heat, I was glad I'd taken time to put on my leather trousers. The sand went everywhere...and I mean *everywhere*.

"It's noon," Ramesses said. "We'll rest in the shade."

"Shade?"

As well as bringing a vast array of necessary items like silver-mounted toothpicks and ivory-handled backscratchers, Ramesses had thoughtfully provided shade. A little persuasion and the camel I'd dubbed 'Nightmare' laid down beside the pile of luggage we'd taken off him. His lumpiness extended beyond the humps on his back. His stomach puffed up and Pharaoh and I lay in the shade cast by his belly. 'Bad Dream' waited patiently, chewing with long round motions of his soft-lipped mouth. I watched him with fascination as the lips transcribed an endless circle, and found my eyes closing.

We traveled with only a few hours pause out of the twenty-four. The landscape changed so little that I found it difficult to measure progress. When Ramesses had said we'd travel to the First Cataract, I thought that meant we'd follow the river. But he seemed to have an unrolling map in his head that noted every ditch and outcropping.

When, however, he declared that over the next rise we'd see fresh water, I questioned him. "Wait a minute. You haven't been out here since you were a youngster and yet you know where everything is. How is that possible?"

"Oh, all pharaohs have a mystical connection with the very soil of the land. We know it as we know our wives' bodies in the darkened bedchamber."

"Do I look like I was born yesterday?" I'd begun to know that he wasn't serious when his mouth primmed up a certain way denying the laughter-wrinkles around his eyes.

"Oh, all right. I can't fool you, I guess. You see that pile of stones? Looks entirely ordinary, right?" He pointed toward a collection of rocks that were, to my untutored eye, exactly the same as any other haphazard tumble. We'd passed a hundred of them at least in the last several days.

"Yes. It's a pile of stones, sure enough."

"Traders pass this way, coming in from the southern kingdoms. When they do, they leave certain signs behind them which inform other travelers of what lies ahead. It's a code as old as time, unchanging and highly useful."

"And it tells you that there's water over there."

"If you don't believe me, ask the camels."

They were poking their noses out on those sinuous necks and walking almost perceptibly faster. When I considered that no encouragement of mine had increased their pace at all, I took this as a sign that Ramesses was right.

"Is this the oasis we've been working towards?"

"Not yet. We will know when we pass the borders."

"I hope you're right and this evil won't cross out of Egypt."

"No one wishes that more fervently than I."

The water level was low, meaning that it wasn't quite as clear as it could have been. The camels weren't picky and neither was I. Though Ramesses had packed well, dried fruit, salted meat, and unleavened bread made for thirsty meals. Nor had he expected me to need so much of these staples just to keep going. After a couple of days, I'd already cut back. I had to be careful, however. Too little food and I'd be unable to defend him adequately.

I did notice that there were several packages hung on Nightmare that he never opened. Once when he was relieving nature, I shook one. It rattled with a clicking noise rather like dice. None of my business, I supposed, but I was still curious.

He never played the king, even though fate had left him with only one underling. He did a full share of whatever work needed to be done, whether picking fleas off the camels or tending the fire. He knew some songs that I had not heard before and was entirely willing to learn new ones from me. He asked me many questions about life outside of Egypt, customs, foods, arts and sciences. I was happy to tell him whatever he wanted to know.

"I have enjoyed being a king," he said. "But it is a narrow life."

"You can't say that about mine," I answered with a rueful laugh. "But I don't think I'd want it any other way."

"So if someone made a spell and put you on the throne of, say, Egypt, you'd refuse?"

"I hope so."

"Beautiful girls, fabulous wealth, the command of armies...these things do not appeal to you?"

"For a couple of days, maybe. 'Til the novelty wore off. I wouldn't much like sparring with men who feel they must let you win."

"I understand that. And women who are only there because of your wealth and position aren't the sort you wish to know."

"I wouldn't go that far," I said.

"My new daughter tells me that you behaved very well to her when you were alone together in the mountains of your land."

"I hope she remembers to tell Smendes that. He's the jealous type." I still had the bruises to prove it.

"Ah? You think he's interested in her?"

"From the second he saw her. Even before he knew she was related to you."

"That relieves my mind. Not having any other marriageable daughters at the moment, I never tested his steadfastness in that direction. There are many men who'll marry a princess, even an ugly, ill-tempered princess, to gain a throne of their own."

"Well, I'll testify Naunet is neither of those."

"I regret I did not spend more time with her," he said.

"There'll be plenty of time when we go back."

"Yes, no doubt. Of course, if you are right, it will not be long before she is given in marriage to General Nesibanebdjedet. You are certain that he feels more for her than mere ambition?"

"It's pretty obvious, can't take his eyes off her, talks about her incessantly, sighs her name under his breath...all the signs."

"And her? Do you have insight there as well?"

"It's harder to tell with women."

"True, very true," he said reminiscently.

"I know one thing. She's not in love with me. At first, she thought she'd like to be, but not now."

"I'm sorry to hear that, for my country's sake as well as for your own."

This was very flattering. It isn't every day someone hints delicately that he'd like to welcome you to the royal family. The more we talked about Naunet, her good humor under field conditions, her bag of tricks, even her refusal to abandon the baby, the more I wondered if I hadn't been too hasty in deciding she wasn't the girl for me. Maybe I'd made a mistake. Maybe it wasn't too late.

Maybe it was just the desert loneliness talking.

"I'm afraid I'd make just as poor a son-in-law as I would a prince."

It was a day later that I realized I had that 'being followed' feeling again. Halting Nightmare, I looked back over the flat, endless landscape. The hot air rising from the desert floor rippled like a dancing girl's hair, fooling the eye. Though the sun had dropped from the zenith, the heat still seemed to increase, drawn from stones and the earth itself. Only later would the temperature drop to set us shivering again.

Very distantly, on the limit of clear sight, I thought I saw a little dust devil arise and begin to spin lazily. "What is it?" Ramesses asked.

"I'm not sure. Maybe nothing. This isn't my land; I don't know what's normal."

"What do you see?" He stood beside me, lifting a hand to shade his eyes.

"Dust. That's all."

"It could be another caravan, late in the season. No reason to think it has anything to do with us."

The dust devil, if that's what it was, faded away. I stood watching for another minute or two. I was willing to accept that wind was capricious, blowing hard enough over there to whip up a mini-cyclone while leaving us undisturbed.

"How much further do you think we have to go?"

"Another day, perhaps two."

"We should rest much less often, I think."

"Because of a dust devil?"

"Because I'm not without experience, which is why I'm here, right?"

He nodded and we walked on. Later on that evening, far off in the direction we were going, a thunderstorm arose. We could see the lightning pulsing through the clouds, though the storm was too far away to bring us the sound of thunder. "That's near where we are going," Ramesses said. "I hope it refills the oasis' waters where my sons are."

We stopped only for a short time and I did not sleep at all. My heart felt oppressed and I brushed at my arms and legs, feeling as if I had ants crawling on me. I knew these signs of old. Trouble was coming.

I woke him up. He blinked in the darkness, unsure for a moment where he was. "We'd better go," I said, feeling a little sorry for him. He was an old man, after all. On the other hand, he did tend to whistle through his nose when he was asleep.

An hour or so after dawn, we passed two obelisks, their carvings clogged and obscured. Tapering, thin, they looked all the taller for being the only tall things around. Even buried to a third of their length in the sand, they towered over me.

"This is it," Ramesses said, his face lighting. "This is the border."

I tensed. If anything were going to happen, it would be now. I waved for him to go on, while I kept the rear. I didn't know what I expected, fountains of sand, roaring beasts, an overlarge Gorgon...

Nothing happened. He trotted through the space between the obelisks as easily as a child running between his parents. There wasn't even a bolt of lightning let alone a crack of thunder. No god spoke from the sky. Ramesses didn't even look back.

I followed him. He turned at last toward the west, heading back toward the upper reaches of the Nile.

We reached the oasis south of the First Cataract by early evening. A brownish tent had been raised up there between two palms, big enough for several people. A camel stood beside it, looking bored but then camels rarely look any other way. Except for the camel, there was no other sign of life.

Ramesses dropped the lead rope and stumbled down the slight slope before us. Nightmare and Bad Dream followed him, eager for once if only to get to know the other camel.

I followed, hand on my sword. The uneasy feeling had been haunting me for days, waking and sleeping. I mistrusted the peaceful scene.

Ramesses tried to speak, to call out to his sons. I caught his arm to support him the rest of the way down the slope. "Take it easy," I said. Then I called out. "Montu. Rudjek? Your father is here."

Something caused the side of the fancy stand-alone tent to bulge and jerk. Whatever was in there was still alive. I held Pharaoh back and went first.

"My sons?" Ramesses called, his voice cracking.

Dreading what I might see, I thrust back the flap of the tent and peered in. A waft of stale air came out. A pale face, drawn with hunger and exhaustion, looked up at me from a blanket on the ground. "I'm sorry. Would you mind repeating that?"

"I said, your father is here."

With one weak hand, the young man pawed at a bundle of blankets beside him. "Wake up, Rudjek! The best mirage of all has just arrived."

"The malachite-green dancing girl with the bouncing ribbons again? I liked that one."

"Better yet. Rescue."

CHAPTER SIXTEEN

I was never so glad to be wrong.

Ramesses, behind me, gave a gasp and melted at the knees. I caught him before he planted his face in the sand. "Calm yourself. They're all right."

The healthier of the two dragged himself out on hands and knees. He reached out a trembling hand. "F-father?" Then he collapsed as well.

"Stay there," I told the other son. "I've only got two hands."

I plopped them down, each feebly supporting the other, and went for supplies. A little water revived Ramesses to the point where he could speak, even if only to say their names over and over, holding their hands. They all wept together like women at a wedding.

Meanwhile, I blew up their fire, shredded some mutton and brought it to a rolling boil with a double-handful of pulses. Even this they were almost too weak to eat, so Ramesses and I spooned the broth into their mouths. It was heartening to see the life come into their eyes and I felt a sense of personal pride when they reached for the bowls, impatient at our slowness.

Their limited stocks of food had given out nearly a week earlier as near as they could figure. "Nor was it much before that," Rudjek said. "A handful of beans and half a lotus root. But a few days later, what banquets were laid before us! The most lavish entertainments of six kingdoms could not rival it. Fountains of wine, mountains of bread, rare fruits heaped like jewels on the breast of the Queen of Sheba."

Montu dipped a piece of bread into the broth. "My brother is a poet, Eno," he explained. "He chatters like a monkey even on his deathbed. My own visions were more prosaic. A cup of beer, an apple, a hunk of cheese. I could almost taste the fruit and smell the cheese."

"Oh, that was me," Rudjek said, laughing. "Sorry about that."

But it was the joking poet who asked after Kemes. Ramesses shook his head, unable to speak, tears standing in his eyes. I spoke for him. "The same evil fate overtook Kemes as struck down your other brothers."

"He was the best of us all," Rudjek said solemnly. "May I meet my end with the same selfless courage that he showed."

"You don't have to go back," I said.

Montu, the younger, made a repulsing gesture. "We are the sons of Ramesses, Master of Egypt. A coward's part is not ours nor shall we listen to such counsel."

I exchanged a glance with Rudjek. He was rubbing the backs of his fingers over his beard. We were all grubby, unshaven, two unable to stand, and I wouldn't back any of us in a race against a crawling infant.

Rudjek said, "You'll forgive me, my brother, for not being overly impressed with my own royal glory."

"What do you mean by that?"

"We are indeed the sons of Ramesses, the only remaining sons. We owe it to him, to our ancestors, and to his posterity...to live."

Montu thought it over. "I will abide by the wisdom of our father. Whatever he wants us to do, I will do."

For the first time, Ramesses spoke. "Show them what I have brought in the red box, Eno, if you will be so good."

Nightmare stayed by his new friend while I untied the rattling box from his appurtenances. It was square, of red leather, studded with brasses, and a pin-lock hung from a hasp at the front. I laid it down in front of Ramesses.

He fished in his tunic for the key and handed it to me. "Open it, if you please."

I spun it around so the boys could see before I flipped open the lid. I peered over the top, though I had a pretty good idea already of what I would see.

The sun seemed to be trapped in the box. A burnished shine came from within, lighting their faces. Glints of sapphire, of ruby, of crystal, reflected in their eyes.

"My personal fortune is in this box and two more like it," Ramesses said. "Gifts from my wives, your mothers, my parents and grandparents. Some from the few friends I have cherished in my lifetime. Nothing that belongs to Egypt, only to myself in my private person."

Rudjek understood at once. Poets are like that. "Then we can go with a clear conscience, for we are stealing nothing from our people but our own selves."

Montu looked puzzled, searching our faces for answers. "What is this for?"

"With these jewels, we can start our lives elsewhere and live them out too," Rudjek said. "You will make a fine merchant, my brother, and I will sing of your glorious wares to every lovesome lady in Punt. They will pay fabulous sums for these things, reset in cuffs or hair-pins. My father will sit in the sun, with his grandchildren on his knees."

"From the lovesome ladies, no doubt," Ramesses said.

"From one at least. My brother saw a maiden most radiantly dusky in a window as he passed to and from the palace."

"She was very beautiful and smiled at me, but I was a prince then," Montu said, a thought sulkily.

"And you shall be a prince in her heart forever. This I swear, if I must use every poetical trick ever created and make a few new rhymes myself."

They were talking lightly and rapidly, too much so for men newly risen from starvation and suffering from grief. If I could have, I would have gotten them all nicely drunk, not to vomiting, but just sleepy. As it was, I had to order them, even Ramesses, to lie down and be quiet. If they were really going to break for Punt, they'd need at least three days of rest and good food before they'd be ready to travel, I told them, scolding like a nursemaid.

I flipped open all the sides of the tent, releasing any bad air that still lurked there. It was very nearly a double-shroud. I only hoped that Ramesses was right, that whatever pursued them would not pass the borders. Just in case, however, I stayed awake. I had plenty to think about even without pacing the perimeter, keeping an eye out for demons or men. I wasn't sure which one would be worse.

I sat down by the fire for a moment at some point. No sooner did I realize who the criminal was then I jerked awake. On mature consideration, I decided that my mother couldn't be responsible, no matter how logically the evidence had held together in my dream.

A few minutes later, Rudjek woke up too. He drew his blanket around his shoulders and walked, fairly steadily, to sit beside me. "Anything left in the pot?"

I'd cooked up a little porridge of lentils, very bland for stomachs not yet used to being filled. "Don't overdo it," I said.

We sat for a while, watching the sparks fly upwards from our little fire. He chanted a poem, with rolling words and a tricky rhythm. I didn't understand a word for it was in a very esoteric and antique tongue. "The story of a prince who lost a battle with a demon. My teachers told me it meant something quite different, some sort of allegory, but I always liked to think of it as describing real events. Princes do lose battles sometimes."

"And other men as well."

"How do you come into this tale of ours, Eno?"

I told him about his new sister, about my problems with Pan, about my various clients. Rudjek was a very good listener. He picked up a stick and drew patterns in the sands while I spoke, the firelight gilding his face, in profile very much like his father's.

"A pity Grandfather couldn't have spent a little of his otherworldly efforts protecting his grandsons. Not that I begrudge his attentions to this sister I shall never see."

"I wondered if something 'otherworldly' was preventing him from helping your brothers."

"Curses come from the gods, so they say. I cannot think how we have offended. Except...."

"Yes?"

"My father divided the Two Lands into two kingdoms, even if one is ruled by a priest. That might have displeased some god or another. A ghost wouldn't be able to contend with anyone very mighty, I suppose. Change a mortal woman's plan for her daughter easily enough yet be unable to change the mind of Ra."

"Would Ra punish a man's sons for his crime?"

"Heavens, I'm no theologian! I had other brothers who were trained in these arts. I'm number forty-one. Montu there is number forty-six. No one ever expected me to be the next to sit on the Golden Throne."

Rudjek scratched his beard. "There's a legend from long ago, that Ra grew angry with the sins of men and sent Sehkmet in the form of a lioness to devour us all. She grew drunk on blood and would not cease the slaughter even though Ra repented of his hasty decree. Only when we humans dyed beer red with ochre, which she mistook for blood and drank of deeply, did Ra come and claim his drunken daughter. He hasn't done anything like that since, no matter how we've sinned."

"It's a good story but not really helpful."

He had very white teeth which he enjoyed flashing. "I agree. Tell me this, though. You have no intention of journeying on with us to our new lives in the South?"

"No. I'll go back to Thebes. I have a job there."

"So you said. May I wish you the best of luck? You cannot go back, however, without a good story of your own."

"I don't see what you mean. I shall just say that Pharaoh decided to...oh. You're right. That might be a problem."

"They won't just let him go. He's a god-on-earth. Nobody walks away from that. Some have been killed for trying it. What you need is a story. Or are you one of those men, like my brother, who shrinks from telling tales?"

"Hardly," I said with a half-laugh. "I've told more than a few and will tell many more, no doubt about it."

"A man who can tell only the truth is as burdened as one who can tell only lies. Yet how narrow is the difference between the two." Rudjek looked toward the starlit sky as clouds began to eat the tiny lights. "What can you say...?"

I can tell a tale as well as any man but no doubt I was badly hampered by my tendency to tell the truth, even if I'm rarely believed when I do. I have not the gift of altering this detail or that to make a more exciting story. If I am brave, I will tell it. If my heart quails, I'll tell that too.

Rudjek, though, was the kind to add those details. It was not the truth that appealed to him but the strange, the interesting, the exciting.

He spoke low, almost to himself. "So you approached the tent, peered in and was struck by a horrible sight. Two bodies, mere wind-dried husks, lay within. Ramesses clutched his side, looking upon the tortured visages of his last two sons, and fell down dead. Weeping for our desperate ends, you buried us in a single grave, somewhere in the vast and featureless desert. Even if you wished to lead a party to recover our bones for proper internment in a stuffy tomb, you could not begin to guess where you laid us in the sand."

"Well, it's dramatic," I said. "Leaves a few things unaccounted for. Like camels. And if you died at this oasis, wouldn't you be buried here?"

"Make my father gasp out a last request to be buried in an anonymous grave. Everything's reasonable if you tell it right. As for the camels, they ran off during the dust-storm."

"What dust-storm?" I asked.

"That one."

I looked over my shoulder. A wall of swirling brown dust was approaching faster than a camel could run. Rudjek woke up his brother and father. Despite my dislike of the tent, it was the only shelter available. Pharaoh hurried to tie down the sides while Montu checked the ropes that anchored the tent in place. The wind was already rising, testing every bit of rigging.

Quickly, I started throwing everything that had been on the camels into the tent, starting with the water bottles. Gods knew if the oasis would still be usable after this.

Rudjek was doing something among the camels. I was too busy to notice what exactly until I too was safe within. The three heads of the beasts lay on the floor, giving me a sick sensation in the pit of my belly, until I saw that they were still attached to their necks which, presumably, were attached to the rest of the camels on the outside of the tent. They lay docilely enough, probably aware on some animal level that only by doing so would they be safe.

Rudjek said, "By morning, we won't be able to move for camel. They always start with just their noses under the tent."

"That reminds me," I said. "Why didn't you eat the camel?"

The brothers looked at each other wonderingly. "It never occurred to us," Montu said. "I guess we could have."

We stayed awake, distracting ourselves by telling stories, hoping the wind did not tear down the tent. It did the best it could, howling and tugging, tearing at the flaps and billowing over the roof. Imperceptibly, the camels inched their way into the tent, bringing a lot of dust and a strong smell of dirty carpet along with them. I began to hope my acquaintance with the beasts would not be renewed once I left this oasis.

In the dun-colored morning, we dug our way out which wasn't easy with hungry camels nudging your arm every other second. As I'd guessed, the round pond that had been blue and clear yesterday was choked with dirt today. Staying on was now out of the question for any of us.

Ramesses suggested I hike along with them to the next village south, a three day's walk. The two young men seemed mostly recovered, though Montu had to sit down every now and then.

I thanked Ramesses and told him that I felt guilty for taking the High Priest's job only to promptly go off in another direction. "Just point me toward Egypt. If I stick to the river, I should be all right. I'll go back to do what I came here to do."

"You have been a good friend to me," Ramesses said. "I wonder if I might ask a final favor."

"If it's mine to give, you shall have it."

"I cannot go into my new life bearing my old name. May I ask what your father called himself?"

"Thrax, after the first of our Thracian kings."

"Then I shall call myself that until the end of my days."

He gave me three smoothly cut gems, two rubies and an emerald of surpassing beauty, each the size of my thumb. "It is little payment enough."

I thanked him haltingly. I'd come to be very fond of Thrax, as I supposed I must call him now. It was a delicate compliment, suitable to the man he'd been, to honor me by choosing my father's name.

Montu and Rudjek clasped me by the hand and called me brother in farewell.

Then they tried to offer me a camel.

* * *

On my own, I made good time. I couldn't help missing 'Thrax' a little bit and I'd enjoyed my time with his sons. One of the drawbacks to my profession is that I don't know the end of people's stories. Will Montu's girlfriend fall for him now that he's just a jewelry merchant? Could Rudjek get his poems published? How many grandchildren would lighten the former pharaoh's heart in years to come? I only hoped they weren't murdered for the gems they carried at the first inn they came to. Maybe I should have gone with them all the way to Punt.

The sight of a stork rising in the air as if shot from a bow took my mind off these melancholy thoughts. I realized that I'd been hearing the rush and swirl of water for some time without it really registering. Cutting across the dusty odors of dirt and camel dung, the fresh breeze from the river revived me. The rich green of the wheat growing beside it delighted my eyes, grown too accustomed to dun and drear.

I waved to the men working in the field and kept on.

Keeping to the river meant that I wandered across little villages where I could buy food or a bed for the night. A much more comfortable way to travel than across the trackless desert.

No one, however, seemed too certain where the border with Egypt lay. Some villagers weren't even sure whether they were Egyptians or not. Most of them had never been more than a mile or so beyond their own villages. Who ruled them, where the border was, these were unimportant matters. I began to keep a sharp eye out for obelisks or other markers, hoping I'd not passed them without knowing.

In the late afternoon on the third day, my pace had slowed somewhat. I'd had too heavy a meal at my mid-day stop, unable to resist the whole roasted sheep they'd been cooking over a spit. It had been the innkeeper's son's wedding day and they'd insisted I share in the feast. Chance-met strangers are lucky. I probably should have stayed on but I'd begun to feel a sense of urgency. I wasn't getting paid to see Egypt on five drachmas a day.

Finally, I saw the monument that I sought. A stone sphinx lay with paws outstretched facing the river. Smaller than the one near the Pyramids, but large enough to be seen from passing river-boat or caravan, it was not the usual mix of beasts. The body, carved with precision, was that of a lean great cat, a lion or a leopard, with a head to match, for all it wore the striped headdress of a high-born Egyptian male.

There must have been a matching one on the other side, though I couldn't see it. What more fitting to mark the divide between Egypt and the rest of the world than the symbol most associated with their way of life?

I was so glad to see it that I felt a childish urge to scrawl 'Eno was here' on its flank.

The notion was fleeting. While I entertained it, I studied the sphinx to determine exactly where I'd mark it, if I were to do such a rascally thing. Which is why I saw the sphinx wake up, massive paws stretching to their fullest extent, exposing claws like scythes.

I must have gasped or maybe squeaked for it opened great green eyes and swiveled its head to focus on me. Instantly it bounded towards me, as if thought and action were the same thing. The acceleration was appalling.

To turn would waste a precious instant. I ran directly at it. Checking its own speed made it slide a little sideways. This perhaps prevented it from judging its next bound accurately. I ran past, feeling the hot stinking breath from the huge muzzle as it spun and hearing the soft, heavy thud of a swiping paw that missed its target.

Pelting along for all I was worth, I heard a disappointed growl and then the muffled drumming of those paws, like the drumbeat that brings the condemned man out for military execution.

My advice to young heroes has always been, should circumstances conspire to encourage you into running away, to run with all your power. Don't look behind you. If you are running, you should already be putting your feet down as fast they will go. If there is something behind you that will make you go even faster than you already are, you aren't really trying.

I also suggest you don't spend all your time weight-training. Don't neglect to take a few runs around the stadium every other day. It may not be as impressive but developing a turn of speed is just as important as building up those sword-swinging muscles.

As my chest started burning, I wished I'd taken more of my own good advice.

Running parallel to the river, I tried to keep to the harder dirt. Mud would only slow me down. Of course, it meant the sphinx could run just as fast.

It dawned on me that, given four feet and its length from nose to tail, that the sphinx should have outrun me already. So, against my better judgment, I looked over my shoulder.

The sphinx ran just behind me, barely panting, ears forward, whiskers a-twitch. Just as I turned my head, it put on a little speed, even running on three legs, raising the right forepaw to slap out at me.

If a kitten chasing a ball of string did it, girls would giggle, small boys would laugh, and even hard-hearted torture chamber operators would say 'awww!'

It's different when you are the string.

I went into a forward roll, just as the uplifted paw shot out. It would have been a clever move had it been intentional. Catching your foot in a hole did not win any points for style.

The sphinx was on me before I could recover. I drew my sword. When I brandished it, the creature stopped, one heavy paw already on my belly. If the claws came out....

"Don't care for bright metal, eh?"

It sat down suddenly on its haunches, taking the paw away. I held the huge green eyes with my own as I got to my feet. It breathed through its open mouth, tasting the air, showing teeth long and sharp as elephant tusks. It stank, as animals do that live on meat alone.

My own breath came hard, a dry, empty feeling at the base of my throat. Running anymore was out of the question and I would have kissed the Witch-Queen of the Underworld for two fingers of dirty water.

It was an impasse. I couldn't outrun it. I couldn't attack, for I had one sword and it had five on every paw. I'd seen the pampered cats of high-born ladies eviscerate cushions with deep kicks of their hind legs. I wanted to be a cushion even less than a ball of string.

"Nice kitty?"

A deep rumble, half-purr, half-snicker, issued from its open mouth. A red light glowed from behind the green lens of its eyes, each the size of my head.

The red light grew, beaming out from the eyes to bathe me in the glow. I felt cold despite the warmth of the color, the hot temperature of the day. My will to move, even so much as a finger, began to be drawn from my body, flowing from me to the demon-sphinx. I could no longer feel my feet, my hand on my sword, or the sweat trickling down my chest.

I knew I was turning to stone like the others. But how could that be, I asked myself. I was not of their family.

Even as that thought passed through my mind, the light went out.

CHAPTER SEVENTEEN

The demon-sphinx dropped onto its belly, paws crossed delicately at the wrist. "Well," it growled, "you are not like the others, Heir of Ramesses."

"No, no," I said. "You've got the wrong man."

Being able to move again reassured me. The insect bite that itched on my shoulder seemed like a blessing, as did my sword, drawn now and gripped lightly in my hand. I didn't know what good it would do, but it made me feel better just to hold it.

"Indeed? Then where is Ramesses and where are his sons?"

"Dead. I buried them out in the desert. The other side of the border. Beyond anyone's reach."

Raising one vast paw, it gnawed intensely for a moment among the pads. Then it licked the back twice with great care, making sure every hair lay properly, before looking at me with the doubting sideways slant of a housecat told that the kitchen is out of fish.

"You claim that you have buried him and his sole remaining sons. I called you the Heir rightly. Did they not tell you that he who buries a pharaoh becomes pharaoh?"

Was that true? Rudjek must have known it. "They must have forgotten to mention it."

"It is a very ancient law. It is the beginning of all the human law in this land. I know, for I am as old as Egypt itself."

"That's awkward. Well, no doubt they'll make an exception in my case."

It laughed again. "No exceptions."

It raised slowly up, elbows leaving the ground, but even as it did so, I raised my sword. It settled down again as if it had merely adjusted position for comfort's sake. The slitted eyes and twitching tail-tip said otherwise.

"So, how is the demon business these days?"

"Same as always. Men ask for what they want and then weep over the necessity of it all. Or they ask for the wrong things and try to undo what has been done. Not even Ra can do that, yet they go on trying."

I've dealt with small demons before, half-formed or who were possessing their first soul. I'd never met one like this. Most can't talk, let alone converse like a symposium scholar.

"Hey, humans, what can you do? I know what you mean. I'm part god myself."

"Which part?" it said and purred at the joke.

"Can you tell that about someone?"

"Are you asking me for a favor?" It lifted its black upper lip in what passed for a cat's smile. The pointed teeth robbed it of charm.

No one with any claim to wisdom ever asked a demon for a favor. But someone had. A big favor which had been carried out. "I'm confused, Cat. Why the turning to stone? Why not just eat 'em?"

"Oh, that." It waved a paw airily.

"Go on. You don't know how interested I am." Even demons like to talk about how clever they've been.

"I thought long and hard about that. Would you believe the human who conjured me up didn't want any of their blood to be shed? 'End the divide,' he bleated. 'Make Egypt whole. Punish him for his blasphemy...' All fine words, bravely spoken. Then the mewling addition of 'but don't spill their blood'. Pish! Typical."

"Turning them to stone killed the men, breaking Pharaoh's spirit but keeping within the letter of the request. Witty kitty."

"One does one's best. I suppose I can't help being artistic about it after all this time. I remember when it was just 'catch 'em and kill 'em quick.'"

"And this person has been trying to call you off for a while now?"

"Since the fourth or fifth one. He hardened his heart at first, calcifying his soul with cruelty and the excuse that 'it had to be done for the good of the country', but he is weak and failed of his resolve." The demon hissed at the memory.

"Is he still trying?"

"All the time. Prayers, incantations, hymns, sacrifices, all the tricks of the trade. They don't work, of course. A curse once incurred must be finished."

"I see." I should have suspected it from the first time I heard he was looking for me. You only send for an outside contractor when all your home-grown attempts have failed. But if the High Priest of Amun couldn't lift a curse of this nature, I should have wondered why. He couldn't lift it because he'd laid it on.

"The High Priest of Amun," I said under my breath.

"What's that?" The demon-sphinx stood up, not in any threatening way. I felt for two obols it would brush up against me like any pleased housecat. "You know, if you say the name of the person that summoned me, I vanish. But of course, I can't give you any hints. That would be immoral."

"You've been running around the desert for eight years," I said. "You must be ready to go back to wherever it is you come from."

"I come from the mind of Sekhmet, for I bear her semblance. She delights in destruction and was glad to lend me for another's purpose." It sighed. "But I long for the halls and chambers of the Underworld, to tumble and chase with my littermates, to usher the dead for judgment as is my proper duty. Time is nothing there. Here, it ruffles my fur and grates on my bones."

It shook all over, like a cat emerging from an unwanted bath. I couldn't feel sorry for it, even if it was acting under a compulsion it was not responsible for. The work it had come to do was done, mostly. I hoped Rudjek and Montu would never try to come back to Egypt. Though I'd send the demon back to the Underworld, nothing would keep it there if one of the heirs of Ramesses returned.

I looked into the deep green of its lamp-like eyes above the blackened muzzle. "I don't know his whole name but we'll hope for the best. Wadjmose, High Priest of Amun."

The wind blew hot from the desert, sending whirlwinds and dust devils spiraling up from the earth. I shut my eyes against the blowing grains of sand. When I heard birds singing in the reeds and smelled the rich mingling scents of river-water and mud, I opened them and found I was alone.

I also discovered that the demon had done me a favor after all. Instead of standing in a field three weary days' walk from Thebes, I stood outside the Great Temple. A procession of garlanded priests and young acolytes was passing the front gate, singing a hymn to the Sun. Seeing me appear out of nowhere, scraggling beard, sword still in my hand, caused several boys in the middle to stumble, throwing the whole parade into bewilderment.

Leaving the confusion behind, I crossed the inner court. While waiting in an antechamber for Wadjmose to finish his late day prayers, I saw Hebnetma pass by. He was glad to see me.

"We didn't know what had become of you," he said, clasping my arm. "Smendes wanted to wait 'til you came back but as we had no idea when that would be...."

"He's returned to Tanis?"

"Yesterday. He's...he's going to marry Naunet. My uncle gave permission and there was no stopping him after that."

"Well, he's an impetuous sort of guy."

Hebnetma was dressed as a priest, no wig on his head, leopard stole, the whole costume. When I mentioned the change, he ran his hand over his shining pate. "I always intended to take up the priesthood after returning from my voyage. The time seemed right. Now that Naunet is to be married and Mother is also vowing herself to religion, there's no reason to wait."

"Is she now."

"She persuaded my uncle to smooth her way into the Temple of Isis. Many widows choose her worship because Isis is a widow herself."

"Lots of changes," I said.

Somehow shaving his head made him look older and not just in years. The impressive gravity of his expression would lend itself well to the solemn celebration of the daily rites. Soon everyone would admire him for his remarkable piety, and all because he could look twice as devout as anyone else without even trying. It was almost a shame he was just as decent as fellow as he looked, for his face would make any criminal's fortune.

"Yes, it's all very confusing," he said. "The rituals of faith are proving a great comfort to me. To know that these are the ways of our earliest ancestors and will serve our uttermost descendants in the same way is a balm to my mind."

"I can see how it would be."

Hebnetma smiled at me with just a hint of condescension, though he wasn't quite as good as indicating that I was a hopeless barbarian as his uncle was. However, without a word, I was reminded that my gods were upstarts, late-comers to a mystery that had been playing to packed houses for thousands of years.

I wondered how much longer before I could see Wadjmose. Would he deny everything? Or would he admit it, believing I'd never be able to do anything about it? If he tried that tactic, I'd take his head. Regardless, how could I prepare Hebnetma for what was coming down on him?

"You're not fully consecrated though, right?"

"Not quite," he said, looking more solemn than ever. "I have to undergo my ritual ordeal. I cannot discuss these matters with a non-believer but my uncle says he may waive the requirement. I would rather he did not do so. How can I lead my brother priests if we do not have these experiences in common?"

"Whatever you're going to do," I counseled, "do it sooner rather than later. You just never know what might happen."

Wadjmose's assistant came for me at last. He bowed reverently to Hebnetma and not at all to me.

"Good luck," I said. "I have no doubt you'll pass all your trials with ease." And sooner than even you want, I added in thought as I followed the pot-bellied priest.

"You are indeed blessed," the priest said, hurrying me along a corridor. "I cannot remember the last time an outsider was permitted within the holy sanctuary itself."

"I'll try to be worthy," I said flatly.

He sniffed like a cautious rabbit. "If you'd care to have a bath and a shave first, I'm sure the most reverend Wadjmose will not mind."

"I wouldn't dream of wasting his time."

He bowed me into the sanctuary, the same 'well, it's only a barbarian' look on his face that Hebnetma wore. I supposed everyone gets like that to some extent, especially when they have their own specialties. Today, I was glad I could back up my judgments with a sword, not just spiritual condemnation, though I had plenty of that ready to go as well.

Twelve men standing on one another's shoulders would not have touched the flat roof, crossed with cedar beams and gilded with symbols of sun, life, and scarabs. Life-sized paintings of the lesser gods decorated the walls in rows, their large eyes seen in profile just as though head on, so that the chamber seemed crowded with a silent pageant that wound around the room from floor to ceiling.

Between lotus-topped columns with gently tapering sides, there stood statues cunningly painted to mimic life. Here were the chief gods, green-faced Osiris who died and came to life again, his tender wife, Isis, their son, hawk-headed Horus. Among them were Anubis, Set, Sehkmet, and Thoth, smiling with muzzle, beak or, in the case of Set, his own peculiar visage.

All were turned to face the high altar, hands outstretched in love or supplication to Amun-Ra, father of them all. He alone wore the semblance of a man, god as pharaoh to be exact. He wore the ceremonial beard and the Double Crown, surmounted by upstanding golden plumes, almost brushing the rafters. One hand was extended, palm forward, accepting the adulation of his children and of the lesser mortals who worshiped him here. His upper body was wreathed in the smoke from two large incense burners on either side of him on bronze tripods.

Beside all this colossal splendor, Wadjmose seemed absurdly, even grossly, insignificant. I saw the lines of exhaustion marked on his face, the wobbling steps of a man pushed to the limits of endurance, the would-be valiant smile as he greeted me. I would have been roused to pity any other man so driven by his office. There was no pity in me for this creature for what drove him was guilt and fear. His futile attempts to undo what he'd done were worthy of nothing but contempt.

"I hope you bring me good news," he said. "I have been supplicating the gods every waking moment for your success until I'm sure they are wearied of the sound of my voice."

"Then you may as well stop bothering them. I have succeeded."

"You...so soon?" He staggered. I was reminded of how Ramesses had fallen when he'd seen his last two sons still living. I did not hasten to support Wadjmose's bending knees.

He leaned on his staff and sat down rather heavily on the steps that lead up to Amun-Ra's statue. "Indeed you are a mighty man, Eno of Thrace!"

"It wasn't that difficult."

"And modest too, as befits a great hero. But come, you are weary and in need of rest. I'm sure a most impressive tale of battle and strife lie behind your simple words. We shall celebrate tonight at a banquet and you will tell me all about it."

"I'll tell you about it now," I said. "I don't think you'll be bored, though of battle and strife there was remarkably little. The demon was willing enough to share his tale."

"D-demon?" he repeated, trying to laugh lightly. I've heard more convincing performances from parrots. "Have you been out in our fierce Egyptian sun, perhaps?"

"A little bit."

"Ah, well, it makes people see strange things."

"You're not making any sense," I said. "Do you deny that there are demons?" His religion demanded that belief.

"Of course not."

"Then why shouldn't I have seen one to speak to? As you have so flatteringly said, I'm not like other men. Neither are you."

"I - I do not feel well. Perhaps we can continue...."

"Pharaoh's dead."

"What?" He gave a shudder than went deep into his bones.

"We went together out into the desert, far to the south. He'd learned his sons, Rudjek and Montu, were at an oasis there, his last two sons. When we got there, they were dead of starvation. Ramesses collapsed, struck down by grief. He lived only long enough to ask me to bury them all in an unmarked grave. I followed his last request."

He opened and closed his mouth, as silent as a fish. I drew my sword and stood over him. "That makes me pharaoh," I said. "That gives me the right of high and low justice. It also makes me a god."

"Yes. Yes." He looked up at me, as if my face were more terrifying that the brightness of the sword at his throat. For all I knew, it was.

"You hated Ramesses for dividing the country, for his weakness. You prayed for vengeance upon him. When it struck his children instead, you didn't do anything."

"What could I do? The gods had judged him. Only they could take off the curse. I implored, I entreated, day and night. I have broken my health trying desperately to atone. These eyes do not sleep. This body does not eat. I am wracked with pain from hours on my knees."

"You never confessed your crime."

"I wanted to," he said, tears starting in his bulging eyes. "I had to think of my position. I rule half of this land. How could I ruin people's faith in the priesthood by confessing? How could I destroy people's belief in the goodness of the Great One? If they knew Ra would send such a horrible punishment, how could they continue to worship?" He was on his knees, hands pressed together in fervent plea, sweat dripping down his face. All the time, he watched me closely to see if I was accepting his excuses.

"You don't know what it's been like, Eno! I mourned every one of those young men, just as though I had been their father. My heart was wrung with every death."

My hand shook as I repressed the urge to slash his head from his shoulders. "You'll confess now, I think. And in public."

"Think, my lord. Think of your prestige. You will be worshiped and adored, first among all. No more scrambling for petty jobs, doing any fool's errands. The power, the glory of the richest land in the world will be yours. Your lightest word not merely law but a decree from the voice of Ra Himself!"

"Don't add bribery to your other crimes, Wadjmose."

I didn't see where he pulled the knife from. It was just there, glittering as he raised it up in the air. I didn't bother to use my sword. One hand flat on his breastbone and he flew backwards to sprawl against the plinth that supported the huge statue.

"And attempted regicide. The list just keeps getting longer and longer."

"Forgive me," he said, his head hanging. "I don't know what came over me."

"I do. It's all caving in on you, Wadjmose. You're getting buried under a landslide of lies and murder. But you know your biggest mistake?"

He just sprawled there, panting like a dog.

"You forgot where you were. Funny, isn't it? Even surrounded by all the symbols of your religion, you forgot you were in Egypt, a land where the dead don't ever really go away. They're always coming back to visit, to see if their family is getting along, to check up on the running of the country, to be sure they aren't forgotten. How many of Ramesses' sons did you murder? Twenty? Twenty-five?"

I thought he answered but he was only chewing on something. His tongue, maybe.

"So that's at least twenty-five souls who have a reason to come back to visit you. You're going to see them every day, Wadjmose. They'll kneel with you at the altar, they'll stand over your bed when you sleep, if you ever sleep again. They'll serve your meals, morning, noon and night. They're here, right now. Can you see them?"

I looked about me with slow deliberation. "I can see them. Look. Like wisps of smoke in the corners of the room, growing ever more solid. You know their names. Why don't you greet them?"

I'd almost convinced myself. I believed I'd convinced Wadjmose as well when he straightened up slowly, sinew by sinew. He raised a hand that shook so much it was little more than a blur to point into the depths of the hall.

I heard a footstep and turned, expecting to see the assistant priest. Instead I looked and felt my own knees tremble.

Sekhmet stood before us, not on her raised platform but on her own two feet. Her long, slim body could have been any maiden's, dressed from high breasts to the knee in cloth spun from gold. The sculptor had given her an elegant sinuousness even in stone. Living, she walked with the absolute balance of a perfect body.

Above her long human neck, her lioness face seemed to make sense in conjunction with that feline refinement of body. Her tawny fur glistened, orange-amber eyes aslant, as she breathed in our scents through her open mouth. Her white-edged ears were pricked forward above a pale amber ruff of fur. She wore a human hair wig, fearfully braided and thick, hanging to her waist. At the same time pure hunting cat and pure woman, she advanced with the single-minded purposefulness of both.

"Yes," she said, her sharp white teeth showing in an empty smile. "Yes, the dead are here. They are watching us now."

I bowed, a little late. Wadjmose only moaned and buried his face in his hands, his nails digging into his forehead hard enough to draw blood.

"I am sent for a reason," Sehkmet said. "My father the god has sent me for I am wronged in this matter. This miserable creature stole my child from me. He claims that he is working the will of Ra, but I say he worked the forbidden rite of Kagemni-Kamundi to enslave my child. For eight years, I did not know what had become of him. His voice was not heard, his face not seen as if he had been wiped from existence. Imagine my torment, my brothers, my sisters."

A murmur rose from behind me, a murmur of many voices. I did not dare to look. Had all the statues come to life for this one moment? What about the paintings on the walls? Had they turned their large eyes forward at last, to bear witness? I have seen gods assembled before. It was a sight I could happily go to my grave without repeating, let alone such gods. I wouldn't mind looking at Isis so much, for she was beautiful, but I didn't not want in the least to see Osiris. He's depicted as green-skinned because he's the only god who ever died and was resurrected. Unfortunately, Isis didn't get to his murdered body quite fast enough and it had really been very hot during the month he'd been chopped to bits and scattered up and down the Nile, all those millennia ago.

Wadjmose raised his eyes, blinking against the trickle of blood creeping down his face. "It's not my fault," he said and I winced. I could have told him that was the wrong tone to take. "Ramesses shouldn't have divided the kingdoms. It's an insult to you, to all of you. He didn't care. I warned him that he'd be punished. He ignored me."

"Make confession," Sehkmet growled. "Lighten your heart, little man, if you can."

"You should put Ramesses on trial in the Underworld," Wadjmose said, huffing in feigned laughter. "See if his heart outweighs the Feather of Truth."

"Ramesses is not dead. Nor are his last two sons. You have not succeeded."

That rocked him. "It-it was never my intention to kill Ramesses' sons. I don't know why that happened. Your demon-spawn, that was his idea."

I couldn't help but make a sign that he should really moderate his language. 'Demon-spawn' to an already furious lioness and goddess was neither tactful nor likely to sway her opinion favorably. But then, I had a feeling Wadjmose's fate was already written in the Book of the Dead.

"Do you deny performing the Rite of Kagemni-Kamundi, the Master Magician, Restorer of the Slain, and Keeper of the Inner Key?"

"I had to, I tell you! I had to. Ramesses was going to ruin everything. I found the scroll here in the library while looking for royal precedents. I only unrolled it a little way, just enough to see what it was. It did the rest itself. It...it bewitched me." He sounded like he'd just thought of that excuse and was rather pleased with his cleverness. He wiped tears and blood away from his face and smiled shakily.

Sehkmet seemed to sink down into a deep knee bend. It seemed an odd moment for physical exercises. Then I noticed that her knees didn't bend the right way. They bent like a lion's.

Wadjmose still seemed to think that he'd negotiated his fate successfully. "I've been hoping for a chance to explain. I never meant for everything to happen this way. Every day, you know, of course you know, I've prayed for a way to undo what has been done. I even sent for this man to solve this problem."

"And he has discovered the truth," Sehkmet said. "When my child was freed, he came to me at once to learn why I had sold him to you. You lied to my child. You let him believe that I, his mother, had connived at his slavery. His anger and his sorrow wrenched my heart. I cried out to Ra for vengeance and He has answered my prayer, not yours."

She had crouched down, her hands on the tessellated floor. Growing, she stretched, her golden gown changing with her body to become a pelt of soft fur. Muscles flowed over well-defined ribs and showed stark on flank and legs. Her face remained unchanged except in size. For she grew larger yet, exceeding the size of a genuine lioness, and continuing to expand until she towered over everything. She made the sphinx I'd met by the river look like the kitten it had been.

Each of her paws was the size of my torso. Her mouth could have swallowed me in a single gulp. Her fangs were the length of my leg. All this enormity of power and bloodthirstiness focused with righteous fury on the puny person who dared to match his will against the gods.

Wadjmose fell back against the steps once more, his confidence running out like sand from a broken hour-glass. "I have been a faithful priest! I have served you well, all of you. I deserve well of you. I beseech the mercy of Ra!"

"I am the Eye of Ra," she said, her voice now almost all growl. "I am sent to punish, to slay, to cleanse. I have no mercy."

She lifted one paw and looked from it to the miserable mortal now on his knees. One claw alone flicked up from the first toe, something no normal cat could do. Wadjmose threw his arms wide, clinging to the base of Ra's statue, and screamed aloud. Another justification, perhaps, wordless, hopeless, mounting into a dispassionate and condemnatory void.

With a strike too swift to see, the goddess stabbed Wadjmose in the center of his chest and pulled back. He sank to the floor, lifeless. I saw no blood anywhere. His hands were clasped to his chest and a look of such horror on his face that it unnerved even me.

I turned to the goddess but she had gone, vanished in the same instant that Wadjmose died. Her work was done.

All the statues, including hers, were back in their places. A faint mist seemed to be lingering in the corners, or perhaps it was just my eyes trying to re-adjust to the mortal world. Yet even as I rubbed them, the mist began to separate, to take the form of men and boys, about two dozen of them. They bowed to me, arms outstretched in humility. Then they were gone, and my eyes were pricking worse than ever.

I took a moment to adjust Wadjmose's face into a more seemly expression before the rest of the priests came hurrying in, drawn and appalled by the scream. Some of them glanced at me suspiciously but with no mark on the body, they could accuse me of nothing. They decided that Wadjmose had simply died of pushing himself too hard. He had not, as he said himself, been sleeping at all well.

Though pressed to stay by Hebnetma, I could see that he was already hip-deep in administrative duties, even before his uncle was cold. Wadjmose would get a proper burial, though all the rites of Anubis would not help him escape the fate he'd already, no doubt, received. They have a very short way with souls who don't measure up in the Egyptian Underworld, feeding them to a nasty hippo-crocodile-leopard hybrid called plainly enough, Ammit, Devourer of Souls.

For myself, I crossed the Nile to look around the famous Necropolis I'd heard about. It was indeed impressive, though I was more interested in the living.

I was greeted cheerfully by two pleasant young men, rather big for their ages, who were just going off duty. They'd only been on the job a short while but had already been promoted off graveyard shift. Takelot and Fjuti wanted me to meet their mothers.

I'd had enough of mothers of all sorts for a while and suggested we seek out a friendly tavern. They were more than willing as long as I was buying. We found a very pleasant little bar right on the river where the beer was good and the snacks were free.

"Did you hear?" Takelot said. "Rumors are flying that Pharaoh has gone missing."

"Really?"

"They say nobody's seen him for a couple of weeks."

"Hmmm..." I drank deeply.

"I heard that he left a note behind," Fjuti said, dropping his voice. "Suicide."

"Well, you couldn't blame him," his cousin answered. "No king has ever been through such a lot."

"I guess Smendes will get to be Pharaoh now. You know, I'm glad. That's a nice girl."

"Better him than me," I said, glad that no one knew that, according to ancient law, I was now pharaoh. I had, at least, buried the story of what had happened to Ramesses. The old pharaoh had indeed died to this world. Let those with a taste for power serve in his place.

I raised my beaker high. "Let's drink to the new Queen of Egypt. Long may her house be blessed."